TAKING
THE
HIGH GROUND

Daily Devotional Readings
on
Holy Living

John Moran

Published by
Bethel Publishing Company
1819 South Main Street
Elkhart, Indiana 46516

Cover Illustration by
Brenda Mann

Printed in the United States of America

ISBN 0-934998-69-8

TO JOHN, JIM AND HELEN

The three children God brought into the home of
Retha and me, who, with their spouses,
have made us proud grandparents eight times over,
I dedicate this book.

TABLE OF CONTENTS

Introduction

CHECKING OUR ATTITUDES

ACCEPTING THE SAVING WORK OF CHRIST

EXPERIENCING HIS SANCTIFYING WORK

WORKING OUT OUR CONSECRATION AND HIS FULLNESS

LEARNING TO PRAY

WORKING THROUGH CHANGE

RELATING TO EACH OTHER

DOING THE WORK OF EVANGELISM

ASSESSING WORLD MISSIONS

INTRODUCTION

TAKING THE HIGH GROUND is a collection of devotional writings designed to prod us to holy living. The book is divided into eleven sections, each containing six or seven readings. These deal with some of the most pertinent questions we can ask ourselves regarding our pilgrimage with our Savior and our inter-relationships with our fellow travelers, as well as with unbelievers with whom we will interact, if we are truly purposing to "take the high ground"!

The majority of these writings were first published in the "President's View" in EMPHASIS magazine (the denominational publication of the Missionary Church, Inc.) between 1987 and 1997. Others appeared in pamphlets as well as in THE HOLINESS DIGEST, PRIORITY newsletter and the former GOSPEL BANNER and MISSIONARY BANNER. Most of them have been edited and updated or else completely rewritten for this work and published by permission. A few were written specifically for this publication, and published here only.

It will be easily recognized that it has not been the purpose of the writer to present expositional studies. They are simply written devotional readings, the six or seven in each section being related and interlaced, but not dependent upon each other. Each stands on its own.

My heartfelt thanks is given to my secretary, Diane Norris, who patiently entered this work into the computer.

It is my hope that the reader will carefully consider the section of Scripture given at the beginning of each reading as a spring board to the question offered. Then think about the question being asked, read the presentation for your edification and have a time of sincere prayer—about fifteen minutes total.

If one reading is covered each day, TAKING THE HIGH GROUND will serve as a daily devotional guide for a little more than ten and a half weeks. So have at it! My prayer is that God will grant the deepening of your soul and a more meaningful relationship with Jesus Christ, as well as a more effective outreach ministry on your part during these next two and a half months. As you read—and as you pray about what you read—you will spend your time reacting and responding to concepts which are designed to challenge your heart toward TAKING THE HIGH GROUND!

John Moran
Fort Wayne, Indiana
July 1997

CHECKING OUR ATTITUDES

Attitudes - "An excellent plumber is infinitely more admirable than an incompetent philosopher. The society that scorns excellence in plumbing because plumbing is a humble activity, and tolerates shoddiness in philosophy because philosophy is an exalted activity, will have neither good plumbing nor good philosophy. Neither its pipes nor its theories will hold water."

John W. Gardner
Quoted from READERS DIGEST

What is Your Attitude toward the Gospel?

What is Your Attitude toward God?

What is Your Attitude toward a Life of Service?

What is Your Attitude toward Holy Living?

What is Your Attitude toward Perceived Problems?

What is Your Attitude toward Serving God?

What is Your Attitude toward Success and the Glory of God?

WHAT IS YOUR ATTITUDE TOWARD THE GOSPEL?

Read: Romans 1:14-17

Inner attitudes invariably betray themselves through outward actions. An interested father arrived late for his 10-year-old son's Little League baseball game. The animated third baseman on his son's team intrigued him. His "infield chatter" encouraging the pitcher and his "let's get on with the game" demeanor prodded the father's curiosity.

"How's the game going, little guy?" he inquired.

"Great!" was his response, never taking his eyes off the batter.

"What's the score?"

"Twenty-nine to nothing!"

"Who's ahead?"

"They are!"

"That doesn't sound so great to me!"

"I know it doesn't sound great *now*," the third baseman fired back, "but we ain't been to bat yet!" Now that is what I call a great attitude!

What Paul writes in Romans 1:14-17 displays *his* attitude as well—a three-fold attitude toward the most important news ever given to the world—the Gospel, the good news of our Lord Jesus

Christ! FIRST, HIS ATTITUDE OF OBLIGATION: "I am obligated (in debt) both to Greeks and non-Greeks, both to the wise and the foolish." Let's understand clearly the implications of this statement. The Greeks of Paul's era, though under Roman domination, still considered themselves the elite. They were "sophisticated," "scholarly," and boastful of their wisdom. To the Greeks, all others were "unwise," rather "foolish." The people groups especially in the north, in what is now northern Europe, were thought of as being crude and uncultured— "barbarians." And Paul's attitude was that he was indebted to all of them!

Whether high-brow or backward, elite or uncultured, scholarly or uneducated, wise or foolish, to Paul, all without Christ were lost! Everyone everywhere needed to be saved! Paul's tenacious attitude was that, no matter what one's station in life, each person desperately needed the message he preached! That fact placed him under an inescapable obligation, and that abiding conviction prompted the second aspect of his attitude toward the Gospel.

HIS ATTITUDE OF PREPARATION: "That is why I am so eager to preach the Gospel to you who are at Rome." The King James translation states it this way: "So, as much as in me is, I am ready to preach...." His sense of obligation created an overwhelming eagerness, a Holy Spirit prompted "readiness," to preach the Gospel to those for whom he deemed such obligation! This drive was strengthened by the third phase of his attitude toward the Gospel.

HIS ATTITUDE OF EXULTATION: "I am not ashamed of the Gospel (of Christ)!" I offer four reasons why Paul could well afford not to be ashamed of the message he preached:

1.   Because of its complete supremacy - Paul well knew there was no contemporary message, whether religious (from Hebrew theologians), political (from Roman legislators), or philosophical (from Greek philosophers), absolutely none, which could change the hearts and lives of people for the better on a long term basis as did the message he preached! The same is unquestionably true today!

2. Because of its Divine potency - "It is the power of God for salvation...." He was aware that his message was extremely powerful! The original word is "dunamis," from which we get our English words "dynamic," "dynamo" and "dynamite"! There was, and is, power in that message to deliver one from the havoc of sin! It had delivered Paul himself, and he knew it could liberate any person who would dare to abandon himself or herself to the Source of that power!

3. Because of its basic simplicity - "...for the salvation of everyone who believes!" The most unlearned among them would come to understand the fact that Jesus died for our sins, was buried and rose from the dead in the power of the resurrection! We can debate, dilute, dissect, develop, or doctrinalize the Gospel, only to rob it of its basic simplicity— "salvation to everyone who believes!"

4. Because of its future eternity - the outlook beyond the grave, the prospect of our Lord's return and reign, the hope of bodily resurrection, the assurance of heaven forever—all secured by the unfailing promises of a God who cannot lie!

Such was Paul's attitude toward the Gospel! What is yours? What is mine? And how are those attitudes, in fact, betraying themselves in our lives? Do we sense our obligation to share His message of grace? Are we truly "ready" to follow through with our awareness of that obligation? Do we realize that we possess the greatest message of hope on record in the world today? If so, let's be on with the greatest privilege afforded to God's people— let's share Jesus!

WHAT IS YOUR ATTITUDE TOWARD GOD?

Read: Isaiah 6:1-8

At the close of special services in an Ohio town where I had served as evangelist, a young man presented to me a nice mahogany piece with carving on it. Sensing that I could not decipher the meaning of the carving, he said, "Look at it again!" I did—and something happened to my focus which affected my vision! I saw the name "JESUS." You have seen the same type of decorative piece. Out of focus, it is meaningless. In focus, "JESUS" can be clearly seen.

I have concluded that most of us Christians, though we do not realize it, spend a good share of our lives not quite in focus. The result is that much of the time, we do not have a very clear spiritual picture of God and His Son Jesus at all! Due to our blurry vision, God's greatness seems cramped. His holiness becomes warped!

Two questions I ask: How big is your God? How holy is your God? Isaiah was quite an ordinary prophet until, one day in the temple, a new graphic vision of God's greatness and holiness dramatically gripped his being.

Isaiah wrote of this incident in his prophetical book which bears his name: "In the year that King Uzziah died, I saw the Lord seated on a throne, high and exalted, and the train of his robe filled the temple" (Isaiah 6:1). He saw firsthand how great and lifted up his God really was—and is!

Years ago, J. B. Phillips shook a few of us in the evangelical world with his book, YOUR GOD IS TOO SMALL. He was so right! I sometimes fear that we Bible-believing Christians have become the most gifted people in the world at very carefully and respectfully whittling God down to the size we *want* Him to be— to the size which will allow us to feel comfortable with Him. Why are we so prone to forget that God is not primarily in the business of making His people comfortable! He is ever at the task of endeavoring to make us useful!

So then, how big is your God? Elisha's servant discovered how big God is. In 2 Kings 6 the sacred writer records that the king of Aram had heard that Elisha was revealing his planned military tactics to Israel. He ordered his army to surround the city of Dothan where the prophet was residing. Early in the morning Elisha's servant arose and, stepping outside, saw the armies of the king. Wheeling around he ran back to Elisha crying, "Oh, my lord, what shall we do?"

"Don't be afraid," Elisha responded. "Those who are with us are more than those who are with them." Can you imagine how utterly senseless and lacking in prudence this sounded to a man whose spiritual vision was completely fogged over? The servant's blank stare let Elisha know that he needed his spiritual vision brought clearly into focus, whereupon the prophet prayed, "O Lord, open his eyes that he may see." Immediately God touched his spiritual eyesight, and the servant "saw" the hills surrounding the city full of the fiery chariots of the Lord!

I wonder how often God's mighty army of angels is all around us, and His presence powerfully near, but we are oblivious to the fact. Our vision can be so cramped by our comfort zones! If that vision is constricted and our shaky faith is only able to embrace a shriveled God, we ought not to be so surprisingly disappointed when He is not nearly as free to work through us as He otherwise would. Should we feel so shortchanged then when He only does little things for us and through us? If, on the other hand, we by an eye of unwavering faith are able to clearly see our God for Who He is, and that faith is able to embrace all of His greatness and willingness to work in and through us, He will do "exceeding abundantly above all we can ask or think, according to the power that works in us." After all, how big is our God?

Just one more question: How holy is your God? When Isaiah saw the Lord in the temple, flying seraphim were covering their faces and their feet and calling to one another, "Holy, holy, holy is the Lord Almighty; the whole earth is full of His glory" (Isaiah 6:3). His holiness was pure, perfect, and absolute! When Isaiah saw how holy God really is, he cried, "Woe to me! I am ruined! For I am a man of unclean lips, and I live among a people of unclean lips, and my eyes have seen the King, the Lord Almighty" (Isaiah 6:5).

With a live coal from off the altar, one of the seraphim touched Isaiah's mouth saying, "See, this has touched your lips; your guilt is taken away and your sin atoned for" (Isaiah 6:7). With that cleansing came personal, life-changing revival!

Are we allowing a clear biblical vision of the intense holiness of God to carefully scrutinize our hearts? We cannot come to such a recognition of His holiness without also seeing our own lack thereof. Such a vision of His holiness will certainly serve as our greatest motivation for seeking the cleansing of His Holy Spirit in our hearts and the help of His presence in our lives. After all, the bottom line to personal revival is to live holy lives in honest obedience to His will, out of love!

How big is your God? How holy is your God?

WHAT IS YOUR ATTITUDE TOWARD
A LIFE OF SERVICE?

Read: Philippians 2:5-7; 1 Corinthians 9:19; Ephesians 6:7

During the early years following my conversion, I remember that the following words of Charles Wesley's hymn challenged many of us young men who were anticipating a lifetime of service to Christ on behalf of others:

> "A Charge to keep I have, a God to glorify;
> A never-dying soul to save and fit it for the skies.
>
> "To serve the present age, my calling to fulfill;
> O, may it all my powers engage, to do my Master's will.
>
> "Arm me with jealous care, as in Thy sight to live;
> And, O, Thy servant, Lord, prepare, a strict account to give.
>
> "Help me to watch and pray, and on Thyself rely;
> Assured if I my trust betray, I shall forever die!"

It seems to me that something of such total self-abandonment to a life of dedication to Christ for the sake of others on the part of Christians has gone out of the fibre and stitching of the typical current day commitment. The former deep hope and longing of so many Spirit-filled parents in evangelical churches that possibly God would call at least one of their children into full time Christian service, in the pulpit or on a mission field or some other aspect of the Lord's work, has been exchanged for "more practical dreams." It is far more common now for "committed" parents to think of their children growing up "to make something of themselves," which usually includes "making a good and successful living." And "success" now is at least subconsciously, if not overtly, measured in terms of dollars and possessions.

If such an assessment is true of the typical Bible believing home (which surely affects the typical church also), what must be said of our curious "Christian watchers" in general? Without a clear-cut challenge from the church, why would their goals be expected to be higher? This ever-increasing emphasis on self-centered values has forced our present society to barter itself out of the narrow arena of willing, sacrificial service for the sake of others. Few would even attempt to deny that the original ideals of missionary fervor withinin the church and the former Peace Corp mentality outside the church, have all but faded! A large "Christian" audience has unashamedly rushed headlong into the wide and alluring field of egotism, materialism and recreationalism. Others have very carefully and guardedly slipped in sideways! But sooner or later they are all asking the same questions: "What's in life for me?" "How much will I make?" "What benefits can you promise me?" "How rapidly will I be promoted?" Realistically, all signs point to the fact that this mindset will not soon change for the better.

Will you and I be effective at all to change this contemporary way of thinking? If so, we must make at least two clearly defined decisions. First, we must decide forthrightly, that we are really willing, in whatever vocation we are involved, to give ourselves in committed service to Christ on behalf of others! Secondly, we must decide *for whom* we will be willing to give ourselves in such service.

And, while we are making the decision for whom we will be willing to give ourselves, we cannot afford to ignore the following five facts concerning the people of our country and the world: (1) Of all the Americans who have lived past the age of 65, nearly two-thirds of them are alive now! (2) 77% of all Americans live in a city or a suburb! (3) The Asian and Hispanic populations in the United States are in the process of increasing by 35-40% in this decade—the black population by 15%. (4) Whereas 65% of the American population describe themselves as "religious," only 19% say they believe being a Christian has anything to do with the acceptance of, or a personal relationship with, Jesus Christ. (5) On a worldwide scale and utilizing the broadest definition of the term "evangelize," fully 75% of our world's population remains unreached! Hundreds of unreached people groups have no church among them strong enough to complete the work of evangelization. They can only be reached by cross-cultural missionary effort!

I ask again, "Will you and I be effective at all to change this?" We will, only if we assume the heart attitude of our Master who the Bible says, "made Himself nothing, taking the very nature of a servant" (Philippians 2:7). Let us, by God's help, capture the spirit of Paul the apostle who wrote, "Though I am free and belong to no man, I make myself a slave (servant) of everyone" (1 Corinthians 9:19), and again, "Serve wholeheartedly, as if you were serving the Lord, not men" (Ephesians 6:7). Even so, Lord, help us!

WHAT IS YOUR ATTITUDE TOWARD HOLY LIVING?

Read: Philippians 2:12-14

Obedience to God does not flow from any of us automatically! When God relates to those who have been saved by grace, He is not dealing with dangling puppets on the end of a divine control string. God is a moral being, and He interacts with moral people— free agents capable of negative or positive choices. Hence, human responsibility is addressed in Philippians 2:12 where Paul writes, "...as you have always obeyed...continue to work out your salvation with fear and trembling" (NIV)—or "...with a proper sense of awe and responsibility" (J. B. Phillips). Here is a call to holy living—a call to recognize one's responsibility to fully cooperate with God!

This is not a call to render obedience to God in order to merit one's salvation. We are saved by grace through faith in Christ alone (see Ephesians 2:8-10); but having received His salvation by faith, we are clearly called upon to *work out* that faith by progressively and increasingly expressing it in our lives. We are to *work out* (bring to completion) in our everyday living what Christ has *worked in* us by faith through the operation of His Holy Spirit. This can become a growing reality only as we "continue to obey" the Savior whom we have come to trust fully.

Such ongoing obedience obviously calls, on our part, for the persistent exercise of the will. "Working out our own salvation" can never occur if we put our wills in neutral. We must continually *choose* to cooperate with God in obedient, yielded submission to His will.

But a further, and most necessary, fact emerges in verse 13 of our Philippian text. If verse 12 calls us to exercise our will in *cooperation with God*, verse 13 promises divinely given capability through *inspiration from God* to all who so cooperate! "For it is God who works in you to will and to do what pleases Him," declares Paul. The human will alone is not sufficient. Here is divine enablement! As our will is kept submitted to God, He begins to operate through that yielded choice process. He breathes into our hearts both the *desire* and *dynamic* to do what He wants us to do! He gives both the *motivation* and the *activation*.

When we surrender our power of volition completely and continually to the control of Jesus Christ, God—by the indwelling Holy Spirit—transforms our very inner desires. Let's read it again: "For it is God who works in you *to will* (that is the desire, the motivation, the power to will) and do (that is the dynamic, the activation and power to work) what pleases Him."

This is not predestined divine determinism! This is not God working in us *in spite* of our will. This is God operating in us *in cooperation* with our will. The truth is simple. When we fulfill verse 12 by continually choosing to cooperate with God through persistent, willing, yielded obedience to Christ, we may fully trust Him to fulfill verse 13 in us. It will be done through the inworking power of the Holy Spirit, infusing into our hearts an ever deepening, driving desire and dynamic to do what pleases Him!

Do we want to live holy lives? Then let us volitionally respond in positive ways to the necessity of agreeing with God—a type of harmony which will manifest itself through a life of total obedience to the will of God as we honestly comprehend it! And let us fully expect God to enable us to render such submission. So help us, Lord Almighty!

WHAT IS YOUR ATTITUDE
TOWARD PERCEIVED PROBLEMS?

Read: John 6:1-13

The miracle performed by Jesus, found in John 6:1-13 is recorded by all four of the Gospel writers. Hearing about the death of John the Baptist (Matthew 14:11-13) and desiring that His disciples rest awhile from the demands of their ministry (Mark 6:31), Jesus withdraws with them to a solitary place. But the crowds, more than five thousand strong, follow. Jesus, moved with compassion, speaks to them about the kingdom of God and heals their sick (Luke 9:11).

The Problem—Late in the afternoon a very pressing problem becomes evident to the disciples. Here are five thousand people—and no food! They offer the most sensible solution they can. "Send the crowd away so they can go to the surrounding villages and countryside and find food and lodging, because we are in a remote place here."

That's it! Get rid of the problem by sending it away! But sending the people away would also limit further ministry. It was the very problem that made possible the ministry! What a utopia it could be if there were no problems. But where there are no problems, there is probably no ministry, either.

His Proposition—Jesus responds, "They do not need to go away. You give them something to eat." Then comes the test. He asks Philip, "Where shall we buy bread for these people to eat?" Philip's reaction is so typical—simple arithmetic! He looks at the people, counts the money, and concludes, "Eight months' wages would not buy enough bread for each one to have a bite." Does this sound familiar at all? Judas may have been the treasurer, but Philip had to have been the accountant!

Jesus presses His challenge. "How many loaves do you have? Go and see" (Mark 6:38). Andrew rises to the occasion. At least he found something! True, it was a very small supply—but let's give him credit for finding something! "Here is a boy with five small barley loaves and two small fish, but how far will they go among so many?" Like so many of us, the disciples "see" the overwhelming need (more than five thousand people). They see the minute supply to meet that need—the five loaves and two fish! But they fail to "see" Jesus! There He is right among them as He is among us today! But their "vision," like ours, is so cramped to the great need and the small supply of human resources that they fail to see Jesus for Who He really is.

His Power—The question to Philip was only to test him, for Jesus "already had in mind what He was going to do." You and I may be very sure that our problems never take Jesus by surprise, either. He always knows what He will do. I often wonder what we would "see" if we would only tap His thinking more often—if we would periodically truly think His thoughts!

Jesus instructs the people to sit down. Then He takes all they have to give, looks up, and gives thanks. There is a fine line between "all man can do" and "the touch of the Divine." Things which would never otherwise happen can happen through God's touch. He gives the bread and fish to His disciples and lets them share in doing what He could have done by Himself. They give to the people. And miracle of miracles, the five small barley loaves and two small fish, when touched by the Savior, are more than enough! All have plenty to eat, and Jesus says, "Gather the pieces that are left over. Let nothing be wasted." Twelve full baskets remain! Jesus has just displayed enough power to meet the pressing need—and more!

Here is our lesson. Jesus wants what we have to offer whether little or much. He wants all of it! The issue is not how much or how little we have to offer. The issue is, can we say honestly that all we have to offer is totally His? Let us truly offer to Him all we have and watch Him make the difference!

WHAT IS YOUR ATTITUDE TOWARD SERVING GOD?

Read: Romans 1:9; Hebrews 9:14

Paul makes one of his "God is my witness" statements in his epistle to the Romans, chapter 1, verse 9: "For God is my witness," he writes, "whom I serve with my spirit in the Gospel of His Son..." (KJ). The NIV, in my opinion, is softer but also expressive: "God, whom I serve with my whole heart...is my witness...."

The obvious innuendo is that it is quite possible to render service to God, but for that service not to be "with one's spirit." In the context there can be little doubt that what Paul is saying here is stated as opposed to what would otherwise had to have been written if he were attempting to merit his salvation through the works of that service being offered to God. Then, as now, far too many who were "striving to be Christians" were tenaciously "serving Christ" in order to pacify their guilty consciences. They made a great deal of noise over their "activities for Christ." It was the guilt resulting from their sins, however, that drove them to pile up so many good works in hope of "making up for those transgressions." Here was—and is—a type of service—desperate service—but not service "with one's spirit."

What does Paul mean then when he says that he serves God "with (his) spirit"? In the previous five chapters of this Roman epistle Paul clarifies that he, and all of us his readers, are saved by grace *alone* through faith *alone* in Christ *alone!* The finished work of Christ on the cross is all the work that is necessary to atone for our sins. When we place our total faith in that finished work, and by that faith receive His forgiveness, He cleanses our hearts by the Holy Spirit and gives us new inner spiritual life! To "serve Christ with our spirits" means then, that out of a cleansed, living heart relationship with Christ, and in genuine appreciation for His undeserved mercy which made such a relationship possible, we render willing spiritual service (worship) to Him!

But I believe it is even deeper than this. Paul was not serving Christ by the mere external performances of the ceremonies of the law, of that we are certain! His worship and service were the expression and outflow of his changed heart, this we also know. But that expression was also passionate! It was born of deep desire. It erupted as a result of an inner drive, a God-given enthusiasm and motivation! Paul asserts that he put his very heart and spirit into the expression of serving the Lord! The NIV is probably right on target: he served God "with (his) whole heart!"

I think it is something of the spirit I used to feel as a young baseball player on the team my father coached. He wanted all of us on the team to put all our hearts into playing "hard ball" with a will to win. I was a fast runner (those days are long over). Nearly every time I was on first base my father, the coach, would give me the signal to steal second. I would put my head down and give every ounce of strength I had to beat the catcher's throw. And when I would slide safely under the second baseman's tag and hear the umpire call "safe," I could hear my father's voice hollering from the coach's box, "That's the spirit, Johnny, that's the spirit!" I was very seldom tagged out at second base!

I believe that is the way Paul served the heavenly Father—with every ounce of strength he had! His motivating drive came from the Holy Spirit who had breathed new regeneration life into his spirit. From the depths of his inner spirit, "made alive" by the Spirit's work, Paul rendered dedicated and grateful service to His God. He simply wanted to hear his heavenly Father say, "That's the spirit, Paul, that's the spirit!"

The Hebrew writer expresses this entire truth in a very simple, and yet profound way: "How much more, then, will the blood of Christ, who through the eternal Spirit offered himself unblemished to God, cleanse our consciences from acts that lead to death, so that we may serve the living God" (Hebrews 9:14). Oh how we need that inner driving force of the Spirit prompting us to serve Him "with our spirits"! Ah yes! God, help us!

WHAT IS YOUR ATTITUDE TOWARD SUCCESS AND THE GLORY OF GOD?

Read: 2 Kings 18:7

A profound statement is made about King Hezekiah in 2 Kings 18:7; "And the Lord was with him; he was successful in whatever he undertook."

Not only was God with him—he was also successful! Is God pleased to have us undertake His work with the attitude that it really "doesn't matter whether or not we are being successful; it only matters that we are being faithful"? Is faithfulness alone actually the only issue with which God is truly concerned, or doesn't He also want us to be successful in our work for Him?

After all, is it self-serving or evidence of pride for those involved in the work of Christ to want, as a result of faithfulness, to succeed? It could be, of course! Ironically, one of the most subtle dangers of sincerely aiming for real spiritual success could surface if one hits that aim. The person involved may discover that it all has been nothing more than a driving exercise in egotism. May God forbid!

On the other hand, it need not unfold that way at all! "Success," after all, is not a Christian swear word! I am totally convinced that God does indeed want us to truly succeed in His work. But success will come only as the result of gearing our hearts and minds to expect it! My father was my first baseball coach. He willingly took on the increasingly frustrating task of trying to bring together a bunch of junior-high ragtags who were full of high spirits and aspirations, as well as varying degrees of budding, but slippery talent. And confidence was shaky. The first lesson he tried to teach us was to always go on the ball field fully expecting to win! "You may not always win," he would tell us. "And when you get beat I don't want to hear you make excuses or whine. Congratulate the winning team and be good losers. But I don't want you ever to go on the field expecting to lose! Always play to win! And always expect to win!"

What advice! What a challenge for us who are members of the Church of Jesus! We who do the work of the Lord are not in this task to "simply give it a good try and see what happens." We are in this work to win! But this is not a game! It is for real! Winning has eternal benefits—losing, eternal repercussions! Our whole aim and purpose is to defeat the enemy—and, yes, to win!

Our mission statement for the denomination of which I am a part affirms that we are committed to "being holy people of God in the world," and to "building His Church through worldwide evangelism, discipleship and multiplication of growing churches...." And we strongly purpose, not only to be faithful in both of these areas, but also successful by the help of the Holy Spirit. But we also state clearly that we are committed to be certain that our being holy people of God in the world and our building His Church will both truly be "all to the glory of God!"

"All to the glory of God!" There is the motivating attitude that saves from self-centered pride and egotistical arrogance. The task is great. Whether it is "being holy people of God" or "building His Church," we are the recipients of Christ's Great Commission to win, build and equip people for the service of the Lord. So, under the guidance of the Holy Spirit, let us clearly recognize our mission, spell out our objectives and set our measurable goals. And let us aim to fulfill our mission and objectives and accomplish those goals, fully recognizing Who really gives the victory! It is success to the glory of God that we want, so let us be in the thick of the battle...to win!

ACCEPTING THE SAVING WORK OF CHRIST

"Before a sinful man can think a right thought of God, there must have been a work of enlightenment done within him; imperfect it may be, but a true work nonetheless, and the secret cause of all desiring and seeking and praying which may follow."

A. W. Tozer
THE BEST OF A. W. TOZER
Compiled by W. W. Wiersbe
Baker Book House Company,
Copyright © 1978

Whose Choice is Necessary for Our Salvation?
How Convinced Must We Be?
How Necessary is it to Be Born of the Spirit?
Will We Truly Realize Our Need of the New Birth?
Can We Recognize God's Full Provision for Our New Birth?
Will We Willingly Respond to God's Invitation to New Birth?

WHOSE CHOICE IS NECESSARY
FOR OUR SALVATION?

Read: Romans 3:21-26

God refuses to violate His own character in bringing the guilty to salvation. In order to understand what this entails, let us endeavor to envision *the character of God*. Whereas God is a God of love and mercy, He is also a God of holiness and justice. He holds these divine attributes in perfect harmony and balance. God could not remain truly God if, for any reason at all, His justice ever tore away the under-pinnings of His love, or if His holiness short-circuited His mercy. But the very same problem would surface if, for any reason, God's love ignored His justice or His mercy diminished His holiness.

It is God's holiness and justice which has determined His basic attitude toward both that which is righteous and that which is sinful. His holiness prompts Him to love goodness and righteousness and His justice determines that the good and the right must be rewarded. It is also God's holiness, on the other hand, which prompts Him to hate sin and evil, and His justice calls for sin and evil to be punished.

From the days of Adam we are brought to understand that, since God is holy, sin must result in death (Genesis 2:16-17). And herein lies the problem—we all have sinned! Divine justice demands that sin must be punished to the full degree of the nature of the wrong incurred. Thus you and I must die, not only spiritually and physically, but eternally! For God to reason, "I will simply exercise my love and extend mercy and freely forgive them," would result in a contradiction of His other attributes of holiness and justice. In such a case His love and mercy would, in fact, totally violate His holiness and justice.

So the question of issue must be twofold: "How can God maintain His holiness and His justice, and at the same time exercise His love and mercy in total forgiveness?" Secondly, and more perplexing, "How can God maintain at all His love and mercy without making a total mockery of His holiness and justice?" In each case, obviously, the answer must be that He cannot—not at all—unless someone could be found who was truly worthy, who could die in our place and thus completely fulfill God's divine justice for us (in our stead)!

Here is the good news! God the Father made a choice from eternity past—a choice to offer His Son to die on our behalf for our sin. Christ took our place, paid our price, and fulfilled divine justice for the broken law of God when He was sacrificed for us! God fully accepted His Son, and His sacrifice! And in Him, He accepted us! Sin's penalty is paid in full! God is now able to forgive sinners and enter a new relationship with the guilty without diminishing His own character at all! He can fully maintain His holiness and justice and, at the same time, exercise His merciful love in justifying the lawbreaker (Romans 3:21-26)!

That brings us then to the whole issue of *the character of mankind*. God will not only refuse to violate His own character in bringing the guilty to salvation, but neither will He violate our character! What then, is our character? God has created us free moral agents—people of free will. Not only has God endowed us with the power of personal choice, He has given us, at the same time, the full ability of *opposite* choice. That is to say, in exercising any positive and proper choice in a set of moral circumstances, it is totally possible to make the negative and improper choice. The actual power of alternate choice is what renders choice meaningful at all. Take away the power of *opposite* choice, and *no* choice is available!

God will not make anyone a child of His kingdom who does not want to be. He offers us the privilege to freely choose to respond positively to His adequate provision for our salvation. At the same time He grants us the complete freedom to refuse to respond positively. God will not *force* anyone into a relationship with Himself. Then the full responsibility of free response to God's complete provision lies squarely on the shoulders of you and me. The Spirit of God will exert all of the pressure He can, without violating either God's character or ours, to convince us to repent and trust Christ for salvation. But He will never coerce us into opening our hearts when we refuse to do so. He will never undermine or dissipate our free will.

So the complete provision of Christ on the cross brings us directly into confrontation with the full *responsibility* of free will (Revelation 22:17). If one chooses to respond positively to the pull of the Holy Spirit, it will lead to repentance and saving faith in Jesus for personal salvation—and will ultimately produce a completely changed life. If one chooses to reject the Spirit's pull on his or her heart, the complete opposite will result. God has already made His choice! The price of redemption is paid! The remaining choice of response is yours and mine. Let's choose well—and be saved!

HOW CONVINCED MUST WE BE?

Read: John 16:5-11

God is faithfully, and continually, calling us to accept His Son as our Savior. He will do everything in His power, short of violating our free will, to convince us that the right response on our part to His call, is to exercise that free will to cooperate with His divine pull and to turn from sin in faith to Christ. He will alter circumstances, close doors, bring people across our paths, allow sickness, thwart our plans—*anything* that does not contradict His character—in order to bring heaven's pressure on our consciences regarding our relationship to Jesus Christ. And the one method He will utilize in conjunction with these occurrences designed to draw us to Himself is to send the Holy Spirit to our hearts to speak directly to us about that response.

This direct approach of the Holy Spirit does not necessarily foster a comfortable and peaceful feeling. It is not designed to do so! When we read in the New Testament regarding this work of the Spirit, we are made aware that people were "cut to the heart" and cried out, "Brothers, what shall we do?" (Acts 2:37). Another time they became "furious" (Acts 7:54). We read that Felix "was afraid" (Acts 24:25) and Paul himself, previous to his conversion, found it hard to "kick against the goads" of the Holy Spirit (Acts 26:14).

But, conversely, neither is the convicting work of the Spirit *designed* to make us miserable! Jesus said, "When he (the Holy Spirit) comes, he will convict the world of guilt..." (John 16:8a). The word translated "convict" means basically to "convince." His personal ministry is structured, first and foremost, to *convince* us that sin is wrong and that Jesus is right—with the purpose that we will yield to Him and trust Him fully for salvation! How we may feel about that fact will depend entirely upon how we respond to the Spirit's voice to the soul. Misery and neurotic feelings result only when we resist His call.

This convincing ministry of the Holy Spirit involves us with three areas of concern specifically: sin, righteousness and judgement.

First, "When he comes, he will convict the world of guilt *in regard to sin*" (John 16:8). In verse 9 Jesus adds, "In regard to sin because men do not believe in me." Obviously, the *greatest* issues of life are not exposed before us when one has stolen, or murdered, or lied, or cursed, or lusted, as repulsive and dastardly as each of these sins is! The issue of issues centers in one question: "What have we done with Jesus Christ?" The Holy Spirit's pivotal work at this juncture is to convince us that our sin of sins is the refusal or failure to believe in Jesus. And that constitutes us as guilty before the bar of heaven as we can ever be!

Secondly, "He will convict the world of guilt *in regard to...righteousness*...because I am going to my Father" (John 16:8,10). He is referring at this point, not to *our* need of righteousness, but to the righteousness of *Jesus Himself.* The convicting work of the Spirit will *convince* us that Jesus is right in all His claims! And the final irrefutable proof that Jesus is right is the fact that He rose from the dead and returned to His Father! The fact now stands firm—Jesus *is*, in fact, truly who He said He was—and will *do* all He said He will do! The promise of His second coming stands firm as well. He said, "And if I go...(and He did), I will come back and take you to be with me..."—and He will (John 14:3)!

Finally, "He will convict the world of guilt *in regard to...judgement*, because the prince of this world now stands condemned" (John 16:8,11). At the cross the sentence of doom was passed on Satan. His judgement day is sure! The Holy Spirit will *convince* the unbeliever that all who serve Satan will reap the same sentence as their leader whom they have chosen to follow.

How convinced must we be? We are dealing with a very convincing God! Rest assured, His faithful Holy Spirit does perform His work extremely well. Deny it if you must. But your denial changes nothing! Try to ignore it. Ah. To no avail! For He does, in fact, do what He came to do! He will convict the world of guilt in regard to sin and righteousness and judgement! Let's be sure we have responded positively to His convincing power, and are truly saved!

HOW NECESSARY IS IT TO BE BORN OF THE SPIRIT?

Read: John 3:1-9

Two men engaged in thoughtful discussion concerning perceived implications which must be involved if one dares to call himself "a Christian." The interchange eventually forced them to the question, "What change must be considered *absolutely necessary* for one to become a genuinely biblical Christian?" The prompter of the discussion replied, "Well, I think it is quite unique for a person to experience a rather dramatic encounter with God in his life; but I don't believe it is all that necessary in order for him to call himself a Christian. It, of course, is quite special—but it isn't necessary!" Obviously, many people would agree.

Just how necessary is it to be born again?

The bottom line answer to such a question must come from the inspired Scripture, not from what we might speculate to be "quite special." The Scripture does not disappoint us. We read in John 3 of a very respectable religious leader of the Jews, a member of the ruling council, who came to Jesus one night for an interview. His name was Nicodemus. He was a Pharisee whose beliefs concerning God were orthodox. Their discussion, probably among other matters, included what must be considered necessary in order to see the kingdom of God.

In the course of their conversation, Jesus made a declaration which startled Nicodemus in two ways. The very *concept* of the statement shocked him! The very *dogmatism* of the statement also shook him. "I tell you the truth," Jesus said, "unless a person is born again (from above) he cannot see the kingdom of God."

Betraying his surprise, as well as his misunderstanding, Nicodemus objected, "How can a man be born when he is old? Surely he cannot enter a second time into his mother's womb to be born!"

Jesus' reply addressed his basic lack of comprehension, clarifying that physical birth was not the issue under discussion, but rather spiritual birth: "I tell you the truth, unless a person is born of water (we all know what part water plays in physical birth) and the Spirit, he cannot enter the kingdom of God." Paraphrased, I believe Jesus said, "Nicodemus, I am not speaking of 'entering a second time into a mother's womb to be born!' Unless a person is born *physically*, water being involved, and then 'born of the *Spirit*,' he cannot enter the kingdom of God." He proceeds then to clarify further, "Flesh gives birth to flesh, but the Spirit gives birth to spirit. You should not be surprised at my saying, 'You (plural) must be born again.'" The fact that in the original this "you" is plural is revealing! "You, Nicodemus, and everyone like you, must be born again!"

We cannot afford to miss the obvious intent of Jesus by this statement. Certainly He was not proposing to establish new theological dogma. We in the church have formulated a doctrinal statement based upon Jesus' utterance, and rightly so! However, when Jesus spoke to Nicodemus, the establishing of a doctrinal tenet was not at all His intent. Nor was He insisting upon bigger and more dramatic metaphysical experiences! Some Christians, it would seem, are extremely prone at times to strain their imaginations to the point of sacrificing their integrity, in order to dramatize to others that God has favored them with bigger and more exciting miracles than most others. What a silly and unnecessary shame to the cause of Christ! In His statement, Jesus was not even hinting at this mindset.

Then in fact, what was His intent? Jesus was simply stating to Nicodemus a very real spiritual fact! Here it is again paraphrased:

"Nicodemus, since a person is as he is, (physical and sinful) and since the kingdom of God is as it is (spiritual and holy), unless that person is radically changed and becomes a totally new person on the inside, spiritually it is completely impossible for him to see the kingdom of God!"

The issue of the statement centers upon possibility versus impossibility, not even permission versus prohibition. Jesus did not say, "Unless a man is born again I will not permit him to see the kingdom of God." Oh no! What He did say was, "Unless a man is born again it is *impossible* for him to see the kingdom of God." To minimize at all the consequence of such a pronouncement by Jesus is to undermine the very authority with which it was given. How necessary is it then, to be born again? It is necessary enough that if one is not born again, it is completely impossible for him to see the kingdom of God, and thus impossible to go to heaven. So I say to all of us, in the words of Jesus, "(We) should not be surprised at (His) saying, '(We) must be born again!'"

WILL WE TRULY REALIZE
OUR NEED OF THE NEW BIRTH?

Read: John 3:1-9 (Again)

Do you, in fact, believe that knowing we have been born of the Spirit is the most important issue we will ever face in life? My very sincere hope is that you do! If so, a very basic question, obviously, must follow: "Just how may we be born of the Spirit?" This same question that Nicodemus put to Jesus becomes paramount! "How can a man be born when he is old?" Today that question is being rephrased, personalized and asked over and over again by sincere seekers after God. Modify the setting, alter the circumstances, update the time and people, and we see the same type of confrontation being reenacted increasingly. Often the same type of shock Nicodemus displayed is repeated as well. As sincere and perplexed as Nicodemus, inquirers are also currently asking , "How can I be born of the Spirit?"

How indeed? It is a valid question. Securing the answer must involve us with at least three facets of truth. First, we must realize our actual need of being born of the Spirit. Secondly, we must recognize God's full provision for us to be born of the Spirit. Thirdly, we must willingly respond to God's invitation for us to be born of the Spirit. We will deal with the first in this reading and with the other two in subsequent readings.

Jesus' statement to Nicodemus (as seen in the previous reading) clarifies the first issue—unless a person is radically changed and becomes a new being spiritually on the inside, it is, in fact, impossible for him or her to enter the kingdom of God. Herein lies our *need*! We must realize our own sinfulness. So long as sin reigns in our hearts and sinning is the drive of our actions, it is *impossible* for us to be part of God's kingdom! That very heart condition necessitates some type of an inward change.

Now why is it that, upon the recognition of our sinfulness, we are so often prone to embark on a type of "self-improvement program" in order to make ourselves feel "right" before God? How frequently one reasons, "All right, I'm a sinner. I'll remedy that! I'll stop my bad habits. I'll stop my lying and swearing, my lusting and stealing, my deceit and hating, and all my other sinful practices. I'll start going to church. I will even give to the church. I'll get baptized and start taking communion. I'll make myself right for the kingdom of God."

Two problems emerge with this type of thinking. First, apart from the grace of God this self-improvement expert will discover that it is all but impossible to "follow through" on all of these well meaning self-betterment procedures. But if he *could* follow through, God could not accept him on this basis, for it is nothing less than self-salvation by works. In Titus 3:5 Paul wrote, "He saved us, not because of righteous things we had done, but because of his mercy. He saved us through the washing of rebirth and renewal by the Holy Spirit...." So "salvation by works" is out of the question altogether!

The opposite reaction, of course, is to deny the problem itself. I visited a dying man in the hospital. Endeavoring to win him to Christ, I assured him, "Jesus will forgive you, sir, of all your sins."

I was not quite prepared for his response. It was stated in a matter-of-fact sort of way: "Well, pastor, that's one thing I don't think I have ever done. I don't believe I have ever really sinned against God."

I admonished him that the greatest sin of all was to refuse to accept Christ, of which he was, in fact, guilty. To this he turned a deaf ear defending his original statement—and died never confessing his sin. Let us all be reminded that Paul in Romans 3:23, clearly states, "*All* have sinned and fall short of the glory of God." We must realize God's accusation. Until we truly recognize our need for an inner change of heart, we will probably not seek very seriously to receive God's gift of the new birth. And unless that change takes place, none of us will see or enter the kingdom of God.

It is no wonder that Jesus spoke to Nicodemus with such tenacity: "You should not be surprised at my saying, 'You must be born again.'" A clear recognition of our need will surely lead us to true repentance toward God and faith in our Lord Jesus Christ for the reception of the inner effective work of the Holy Spirit in new birth! So let us forthrightly, first, admit our need!

CAN WE RECOGNIZE
GOD'S FULL PROVISION FOR OUR NEW BIRTH?

Read: John 3:10-17

If one truly desires to be born again, that person must certainly realize his need. We considered this in our last reading. But that seeker must also recognize *God's full provision* for us to be born again. To only be made aware of our need could abandon us to despair if that were the end of the issue. But thanks be to God, that is not the final note!

Nicodemus, listening to Jesus' response to his first question ("How can a man be born when he is old?") obviously could not fathom how a person who had already been born physically (of water) could be "born again." Nor does it seem that he could quite grasp how this second type of birth was not the same as "flesh (giving) birth to flesh." Jesus clarified to him that it was, rather, "the Spirit (giving) birth to spirit." And Nicodemus reacted in the very manner we might expect, sincere as he was: "How can this be?"

In response to that question, Jesus opened to Nicodemus the adequate provision of the Heavenly Father for sinful people: "No one has ever gone into heaven except the one who came from heaven—the Son of Man. Just as Moses lifted up the snake in the wilderness, so the Son of Man must be lifted up, that everyone who believes in him may have eternal life" (John 3:13-15). Then He spoke to Nicodemus what has come to be the most often quoted verse of the New Testament, verse 16: "For God so loved the world that he gave his one and only Son, that whoever believes in him shall not perish but have eternal life." Finally, lest Nicodemus still misunderstand the purpose for His coming, Jesus wiped away all doubts: "For God did not send his Son into the world to condemn the world, but to save the world through him" (John 3:17).

Whether or not Nicodemus fully understood all that Jesus spoke on that occasion, we obviously, cannot be sure. I am, on the other hand, very certain that many otherwise well educated people today do not understand the truth revealed here at all either. Let's reconstruct the scene in more understandable terms. The essence of the question for Nicodemus is this: "If one cannot see the kingdom of God unless he is born again, and if you are not speaking of physical birth in the flesh but a spiritual birth by the Spirit, how can all this be possible?"

The answer of Jesus, paraphrased, is clear: "It is possible, Nicodemus, because God sent His Son into the world. And He will be lifted up upon a cross and die for the sins of the whole world. Now the Father can give you eternal life, though you do not deserve it, if you believe in Me." What otherwise would have been completely impossible because of our sin is now made possible through Christ. When He was lifted up on the cross, it was for all of us. His crucifixion paid the price for our sins. He died for us, in our place. God can now remain just and, at the same time treat us as though we have never sinned. Without violating His own holy character, He can pardon the guilty, because the price for our sin is fully paid and the punishment transferred to Jesus!

So now, through the adequate provision of the cross of Christ, we may be "born again!" We may come to God through Christ and trust Him to work in us the divine transaction of new birth, the work of the Spirit performed in the hearts of repentant believing sinners, whereby we are made new creations in Christ. He breathes into our inner being spiritual life! On the inside we become brand new people!

The fact is, a human being cannot effect that change in his or her own heart. It is the supernatural work of God by His Spirit. We may not be able to fully explain in detail how all of the various phases of the new birth transpire. Jesus said, "The wind blows wherever it pleases. You hear its sound, but you cannot tell where it comes from or where it is going. So it is with everyone born of the Spirit" (John 3:8). We can, on the other hand, experience it all in our hearts! Let us recognize the full provision of God, through Christ, which makes this possible!

WILL WE WILLINGLY RESPOND
TO GOD'S INVITATION TO NEW BIRTH?

Read: John 3:16-18

If one truly desires to be born again, that person must not only realize his need and recognize the Heavenly Father's provision, but also volitionally *respond to God's invitation*. He or she must simply, but very personally, answer God's call to Himself.

I talked to a man some years ago who did not profess to be a Spirit born Christian. I inquired, "Wouldn't you like to be a Christian?"

"Yes, I would," he responded.

"Then why don't you repent and trust Christ?" I asked.

His answer: "Well, maybe someday it will happen. I guess when God gets ready He will save me." The insinuation was that God wasn't quite ready to save him yet.

Now that is the complete flip side of the philosophy of the person who sets out to "work himself or herself into salvation." The one says, "I don't need God. I'll do my own work." The reply of the other: "I surely need God, but I'll have to wait until He is ready." The fact is, God has long since been ready! He has explicitly demonstrated His complete willingness to save us when He allowed His only Son to be sacrificed on the cross. The real issue is, "When will *we* be ready?" The problem is not couched in the fact that God is not willing to invite and receive. The problem is that we are not willing to respond to God's invitation to come!

God has created us free moral agents. He has invested in us the power of choice and the power of opposite choice. He has made adequate provision for our salvation through the death of His Son on the cross. But the personal choice of acceptance or rejection of that provision is left to us ourselves. We may freely choose to reject all that the Father has done for us provisionally through Christ. And God will accept that choice! Or we may elect to turn away from our sins to Jesus and, confessing that we cannot save ourselves, choose to believe fully in the provision of God through the death of His Son! Such a complete change of attitude toward sin and toward God constitutes "repentance."

After explaining to Nicodemus that He must be lifted up on the cross, it is recorded in John 3:18 that Jesus said, "Whoever believes in him (God's Son) is not condemned...." He had already stated in verse 16, "...whoever believes in him shall not perish but have everlasting life." The only way the repentant sinner can come to the point of actually receiving God's offer is *by faith*. He must, in total trust, simply but very confidently, receive from God what He has duly promised in His Word. Faith says, "I do now receive Jesus Christ as my Savior and I fully believe that, by His Spirit, He makes me new!"

It is at this pivotal point of faith that the true victory is either won or lost. It is here that assurance of salvation will begin to blossom or else doubt will continue to shroud the heart. Faith dares to believe that God's promise is as dependable as God Himself. It declares, "I do now believe God's promises in His Holy Word and I believe Christ accepts me now! On the authority of those promises, I know I am now born again." And, as faith relinquishes the struggle and rests in the reliability of the Scripture and the finished work of Christ on the cross, the Holy Spirit will respond to the inner heart and whisper His direct certainty to the soul. By His own direct witness, He will assure the believing one that he or she is now an accepted child of God—born again!

Jesus said to Nicodemus, "You should not be surprised at my saying, 'You (plural) must be born again.'" No, Nicodemus should not have been surprised—nor should we! Our need is profound! Let us realize it! The provision God has made through His Son is full and complete! He can maintain His justice while pardoning us, for His death on the cross has fulfilled all that justice required. His open invitation now stands. Let us respond in repentant faith— and be born again!

EXPERIENCING HIS SANCTIFYING WORK

"God puts His disapproval on human experience when we begin to adhere to the conception that sanctification is merely an experience, and forget that sanctification itself has to be sanctified (see John 17:19). I have deliberately to give my sanctified life to God for His service, so that He can use me as His hands and His feet."

Oswald Chambers
Taken from
MY UTMOST FOR HIS HIGHEST
By Oswald Chambers
Copyright © 1935 by Dodd Mead & Co.
Renewed © 1963 by
Oswald Chambers Publications Assn. Ltd.
Used by permission of
Discovery House Publishers, Box 3566,
Grand Rapids, MI 49501.
All rights reserved.

Who Can be Initially Sanctified?
How Necessary is Dying to Self in the Sanctifying Work?
Can We be Sanctified Through and Through?
How Can We Be Filled with the Sanctifying Spirit?
How Free Can the Sanctified Be?
What of the Process of Continual Sanctification?
When Will Sanctification be Final?

WHO CAN BE INITIALLY SANCTIFIED?

Read: 2 Thessalonians 2:13-14

Spiritual life is always generated by the sanctifying work of the Holy Spirit! In 2 Thessalonians 2:13-14 Paul states, "But we ought always to thank God for you, brothers, loved by the Lord, because from the beginning God chose you to be saved through the sanctifying work of the Spirit and through belief in the truth...that you might share in the glory of our Lord Jesus Christ."

What then, is involved in "the sanctifying work of the Spirit"? The basic meaning of the word "sanctify," as used in the New Testament, is "to separate from the sinful and/or the secular and to set apart for a sacred purpose; to cleanse; to purify; to make holy." In one sense anything can be sanctified. The vessels of the Old Testament temple as well as the temple itself were "set apart" for holy use. Everyday circumstances can be so "sanctified" by the sovereign purpose of God as to effect spiritual strength and growth in our lives. Special days can be "sanctified for a holy use."

Paul, however, in the scriptural text setting above does not envision "things" or "days" or "events." He refers to people and to our heart and life experiences. He speaks of "experiential sanctification" as it affects the inner spiritual heart condition and the outward daily living of the recipients of the Holy Spirit's separating and purifying work.

So what precisely does this experiential aspect of "the sanctifying work of the Holy Spirit" encompass? It is necessary to respond to this question with seven perspectives quite clearly in focus. We will consider the first perspective in this reading. The remaining six we will unravel in the following six readings of this section. We will find that the total work of sanctification does, in fact, embrace the entire scope of the work of the Holy Spirit.

INITIAL SANCTIFICATION—First, precisely who is it who can be initially sanctified? The initial aspect of the Spirit's work in the heart of an individual results in that person being "born of the Spirit." When a sinner responds to the convincing influence of the Father and turns from his sins to God in repentant faith, fully trusting Christ's forgiveness and salvation, in an instant the Holy Spirit executes a work of divine grace in that person's inner being. He is born again (John 3:3). He is baptized by the Spirit into the body of Christ (1 Corinthians 12:13). In that moment the great sanctifying work of the Holy Spirit begins in his heart! He is separated from his sins and becomes God's child and property—to that degree he is "sanctified." I choose to call this INITIAL SANCTI-FICATION.

Obviously, this is not sanctification in its fullness, nor in its final stages. This is sanctification in its initial stage. The Holy Spirit has only begun a good work in the new Christian's heart and life. Paul wrote a letter to a group of Christians in Corinth—a group who certainly were not fully sanctified. Jealousy, quarrel-ing and divisions characterized them, and Paul penned a major portion of this letter to correct these carnal attitudes which were erupting in shameful actions. But in his first letter to these very people, he addressed them as "the church of God in Corinth...those sanctified in Christ Jesus and called to be holy" (1:2). In 1 Corinthians 6:11, after describing the type of sinfulness in which some of these Christians had participated before coming to faith in Christ, he asserts, "But you were washed, you were sanctified, you were justified in the name of the Lord Jesus Christ and by the Spirit of our God." I repeat, here is initial sanctification! It is just the beginning stage and only partial in nature.

But at this point it, is safe to say that though one's spiritual relationship to Christ is established, it soon becomes evident as with those at Corinth that strong inner tendencies still drive the heart in a direction contrary to God's will. These deep inner drives of the heart, anti-God in nature and not yet fully under the Spirit's control, become more apparent to the Christian, ironically, the more sincerely he endeavors to love and serve his Savior. So long as God's will does not challenge the cravings of the heart, all proceeds well. But at the point at which the desires of the heart directly conflict with one's recognized duty to God's will, an inner tug-of-war ensues.

Now we're faced with another question which demands a response: "Is this work of initial sanctification the best the Spirit can do for the Christian?" The answer is "Certainly not!" He has just begun His work. That work is foundational, solid and secure. But it is only the initial stage of what God desires to work in the heart. More is clearly promised and available. That brings us to a second aspect of the sanctifying work of the Spirit which we will look at in our next reading.

HOW NECESSARY IS DYING TO SELF IN THE SANCTIFYING WORK?

Read: Galatians 2:20; Romans 6:6

A second aspect of what is involved in the sanctifying work of the Holy Spirit includes being "crucified with Christ." The New Testament opens our understanding to the need for Christians to completely yield themselves to God, even to the point of an inner death or crucifixion. The believer must die to self. This thought is always presented in the Bible in relationship to the death and crucifixion of our Lord Jesus Christ (Galatians 2:19-20; 6:14; Romans 6:1-6). It conditions our hearts concerning what must be our attitude toward our fleshly sinful nature (Galatians 5:24; Romans 6:7-11). Such an inner attitude of dying to self is presented as the conditional preparation for being able to live the full resurrected life! So we can hardly speak of dying with Christ apart from also considering the fullness of resurrection life through Him.

For our minds to fully understand the implications of what our hearts experience when we "die to self," we must first appreciate the biblical principle involving our identification with Christ in His death on the cross. When Jesus died on the cross, He not only died as our redeemer, He also died as our substitutionary representative. He died "in our place." And in Christ, God saw and accepted us as being crucified with His Son. Our position in heaven, in the mind of the Father, is that of a person who has been, and is, crucified together with Christ on His cross. This is PROVISIONAL SANCTIFICATION, and also involves POSITIONAL SANCTIFICATION.

That is what Paul meant in Galatians, chapter 2, verse 20 when he wrote, "I have been crucified with Christ." Not only had his dependence on the law for justification been done away with, but his very former "I," the former total person he used to be, was also crucified in the mind of God. In Romans 6:6 he declared, "For we know that our old self was crucified with Him." In this verse, the phrase "our old (former) self," refers to our former sinful self, including all that we used to be by nature and by action. More specifically, it includes our self-centered, sinful nature which prompted us to be our old (former) sinful selves.

But this positional aspect of our relationship with Christ, this identification of our old self with Christ on His cross in the mind of God, must also be translated into our own very personal encounter with Him in our hearts. What has been our position in heaven through the Father's choice must now become our own personal experience here on earth through our choice! When Paul writes, "I no longer live," in Galatians 2:20, he envisions that the "I" that used to live—the former "I," the self-centered "I"—now actually no longer lives! He had renounced what he used to be as a result of his sinful nature! He fully consented for that "self" to die. What the heavenly Father saw in a provisional sense when His Son died on the cross, Paul now experienced personally.

Our immediate question then must be, "How can we really, experientially, die to self? How can we, in reality, so renounce our former self that we consent for this self-centered, sinful aspect of ourselves to thus be crucified?" Paul makes a very practical and revealing statement in Romans 6:10-11. He refers to Christ's death first: "The death He died, He died to sin once for all; but the life He lives, He lives to God." Then he applies the example of Christ's death and resurrection to us and says, "In the same way, count yourselves dead to sin but alive to God in Christ Jesus."

From this very practical standpoint, for us as Christians to "die to self," we must exercise a complete inner change of attitude. First we must simply, but very sincerely, count (reckon) ourselves to be "dead beings" to our former selves and the drives of our sinful nature. We must reckon ourselves to be totally unresponsive to those evil drives and desires. Secondly, rather than yielding the parts of our bodies to the sinful nature performing wickedness as we formerly have done, we must now, as those who have been made alive spiritually, totally yield the parts of our bodies to God. Such consecration to God will result in those parts being used "as instruments of righteousness unto holiness" in a newly resurrected and sanctified life!

Following then our initial yielding to God in such a "death to self-reckoning," we must develop an attitude of yieldedness, continuing to yield at every new and more complete understanding of God's will. Any time we fail to yield to God, our sinful nature can rise up again and pull us back to a life of disobedience. Only by a continual attitude of faith in God can we live out daily the fullness of the sanctified, victorious, resurrected life in and through Christ Jesus our Lord and the power of His indwelling Holy Spirit. May the Lord of heaven help us here on earth to experience continually in our hearts what is already ours positionally in the divine heart and mind of God in heaven!

CAN WE BE SANCTIFIED THROUGH AND THROUGH?

Read: 1 Thessalonians 5:23; 1 Peter 1:1-2

In 1 Thessalonians 5:23 Paul prays, "May God Himself, the God of peace, sanctify you through and through. May your whole spirit, soul and body be kept blameless at the coming of our Lord Jesus Christ." Peter affirms that we "have been chosen according to the foreknowledge of God the Father, through the sanctifying work of the Spirit, for obedience to Jesus Christ and sprinkling by His blood...."

In our previous two readings we have considered the sanctifying work of the Spirit from two standpoints: the Spirit's work in the heart of an individual which results in that person being "born of the Spirit" (I call that "initial sanctification"), and the Christian's response to the scriptural concept of "being crucified with Christ" ("provisional and/or positional sanctification" becoming "experiential sanctification").

Now we will investigate yet a third aspect of the sanctifying work of the Spirit which I choose to call EFFECTUAL SANCTIFICATION (or being sanctified through and through). This phase of sanctification is closely associated with and results from one "being crucified with Christ," and involves a deeper work of the Spirit, culminating in the born again person being "filled with the Spirit." A careful study of the Word of God reveals quite clearly that not all Christians are full of the Holy Spirit. It is one thing to be born of the Spirit—it is quite another matter to be filled with the Spirit.

John the Baptist declared of the coming Messiah, "He will baptize you with the Holy Spirit and with fire" (Matthew 3:11). It was the fulfillment of this promise regarding the Holy Spirit's descent on the 120 believers on the day of Pentecost that Luke wrote of in Acts 2:4, "All of them were filled with the Holy Spirit." John's depiction is that of "baptism." Jesus is the One Who will administer the baptism and the Holy Spirit is the agent with which the baptism will be performed. He presents Jesus, the Holy Baptizer, as pouring out the Holy Spirit and immersing the believer, not in water but in the very fullness of the Spirit's holy presence and person. The concept of Luke's statement is that of "filling to fullness" and describes the fulfillment of John's promise by stating that the Holy Spirit filled the hearts of the recipients to overflowing with His presence. Thus, they were to be totally in the Spirit, and the Spirit was to be fully in them!

This is not at all to insinuate that, until so baptized and filled, Christians do not really have the Holy Spirit. Not at all. The Holy Spirit resides in the heart of every born again believer (Romans 8:9). According to 1 Corinthians 12:13, the believer has, in fact, already been "baptized" by the Spirit into the one body of Christ. Thus the picture and illustration of baptism is also used, but with a different intent. The question then that begs response is this: If the Holy Spirit already inhabits the heart of a believer, what constitutes the necessity for Him to "come again" to that believer's heart? The answer is found in the operation He comes to perform on each occurrence. Here is a more extensive "baptism"—with the fire of the Holy Spirit. When a Christian is filled with the Spirit, the Spirit comes in a more complete measure where He already dwells to perform a deeper work of God's grace in the heart than when He breathed into him spiritual life at the moment of new birth. He activates a deeper work of cleansing than that received at conversion.

His work at this juncture is directed more toward the inner sinful nature and anti-God antagonisms which are resident in the believer's heart, and which have doubtless resulted in a pathetic lack of spiritual power. I do not believe this work of the Spirit involves what some would refer to as "total eradication." That concept is simply too strong. It is much more an issue of the counteracting and dispelling action of the Holy Spirit. As light counteracts and dispels darkness, so the agape love of God which is poured out into one's heart by the Holy Spirit (Romans 5:5) counteracts and dispels the anti-God drives and antagonisms resulting from the sinful nature. The aim of the infilling and baptism with the Holy Spirit is to bring those drives of the heart under the strong control of the Holy Spirit and into loving harmony with the understood will of God (Romans 12:2)! And the inner tug-of-war thus also comes under His control.

Further, the Spirit's infilling brings spiritual power! Such fullness is designed to empower the Christian to *be* what God wants him or her to be and to *do* as God wants him or her to do (Acts 1:8), i.e. to be His effective witnesses!

Paul's request to God in his carefully worded prayer recorded above is offered on behalf of believing Christians. It is a plea certainly for more than initial sanctification which they had received at conversion. Here is a petition for effectual sanctification, "through and through." Let the born again Christian consecrate himself to his God in complete surrender (Romans 12:1-2), and let him open his heart in implicit faith for the infilling of the Holy Spirit. In answer to believing prayer, the Spirit will come to fill the yielded trusting child of God with the fullness of His very sanctifying presence. This fullness will then certainly affect one's freedom of soul and one's spiritual progress in daily living. We will consider these very important aspects of the sanctifying work of the Spirit in our next readings.

HOW CAN WE BE FILLED
WITH THE SANCTIFYING SPIRIT?

Read: Acts 9:10-19

Wherever biblical revival takes place, inevitably it is accompanied by a parallel thirst for the inner work of the Holy Spirit. So it must be encouraging to all who long to see such renewal (though possibly accompanied by some excesses) that a great increasing interest in the work of the Holy Spirit has prevailed for a number of years among people all across our country. In every denomination, sincere people of God are inquiring, "How may I be filled with the Spirit?"

I repeat from our last reading we dare not presume for a moment by such a question that a Christian does not have the Holy Spirit. Paul wrote in Romans 8:9, "...if anyone does not have the Spirit of Christ, he does not belong to Christ." On the other hand, we cannot read the New Testament with an open mind without being compelled to conclude that, though every Christian has the Holy Spirit living in his/her heart, not every Christian is "filled with the Spirit." We are also constrained to understand, however, that every believer can and should experience such fullness.

So the question is, "How?" We must consider at least three thoughts if we are to adequately respond to this inquiry.

First, if one desires to be filled with the Spirit, that person must recognize his/her personal need for such fullness. The most obvious indication of such need, especially in light of Acts 1:8, is a persistent marked lack of inner spiritual power. This may become especially conspicuous at the point of some specific temptation which the Christian seems helpless to conquer. Selfishness and self-centeredness may continually dominate decisions. A persistent incapability of sharing one's faith effectively may be a constant plague. Though a Christian, one may experience so *little* inner Holy Spirit power—such spiritual impotence!

Another rather clear indication of this lack of power is a distinctly divided heart. When a Christian, knowing—and possibly wanting—the will of God, is propelled in the opposite direction from that will by catering to evil desires, James would call that person "a double minded man, unstable in all he does" (James 1:8).

When one's own desires and will conflict with God's desires and will, the question of all importance must be, "Who will be in control?" So long as the heart is thus divided, the Holy Spirit cannot be in full control.

Secondly, if one desires to be filled with the Spirit, every hindrance to such fullness and power must be removed. Where there has been disobedience to the Savior, full confession must be offered to Him! Positive obedience must replace that disobedience (Acts 5:32). One must be "confessed up-to-date" and obeying the Lord.

Further, the Christian must face the specific inner areas of unyieldedness and stubbornness very honestly. He or she must take sides against selfishness and arrogance, dealing forthrightly with any unwillingness to conform to the Word of God in any way. All attitudes of the inner heart which insist upon embracing anything or anyone ahead of Christ must be radically altered. Jesus must be enthroned in the heart as Lord over all! The Christian must willingly yield all he presently knows of himself to all he knows of God at this point in his life.

The believer will find that the most sensible course of action to be taken—the most satisfying, safest and most fulfilling—is to totally consecrate oneself to God as "a living sacrifice," as Paul urges in Romans 12:1-2. By removing the hindrances to such consecration, the person's living sacrifice will be "holy" and "pleasing to God" which is his "reasonable service" or "spiritual act of worship!"

Thirdly, if one desires to be filled with the Spirit, he/she must volitionally receive the promise of such fullness. Jesus said in Luke 11:13, "If you then, though you are evil, know how to give good gifts to your children, how much more will your Father in heaven give the Holy Spirit to those who ask him." While this promise includes other areas of need to which the Holy Spirit desires to minister, it certainly embraces His sanctifying infilling also!

But Luke's context would also indicate that the child of God must ask persistently and confidently. God, in answer to His promise, will fill the open receiving heart with His Spirit by faith! He will not fill every heart in exactly the same manner. But when the Holy Spirit comes, He will bring His assurance, His fullness, His power and His purity!

Upon receiving the promise of such fullness, it is essential, then, to "keep on receiving the Spirit." Paul writes in Ephesians 5:18, "Be filled (literally, keep on being filled) with the Spirit." By keeping one's consecration updated and maintaining a receptive attitude toward the Holy One, the Spirit-filled Christian will be enabled to express increasing joy (Acts 13:52), exercise purified motives (Acts 15:8,9) and utilize spiritual power (Acts 1:8). He will assuredly enjoy increased love for God and others and an increasing evidence of the fruit of the Spirit in his life (Galatians 5:22).

Let each of us ask ourselves sincerely, "Am I truly filled with the Holy Spirit?" If affirmative, let us then be sure we are living and walking daily in that fullness!

HOW FREE CAN THE SANCTIFIED BE?

Read: Galatians 5:1-6; John 8:31-36

Freedom! The concept is so powerful and compelling! The reality can be so elusive. How does the sanctifying work of the Spirit affect our freedom?

Referring directly to the Mosaic law, Paul asserts, "It is for freedom that Christ has set us free. Stand firm, then, and do not let yourselves be burdened again by a yoke of slavery" (Galatians 5:1).

The English word "free," among other variously slanted definitions, means "to set loose from everything that restrains or restricts, to be unconfined, unrestricted and unrestrained." But, can we obligate Paul to such an all encompassing application of this idea of freedom when he addresses the subject of Christian experience as in our text? I think not. It is too indiscriminate.

We used to sing exultantly (I don't hear it at all any more), "Free from the law, O happy condition." By such a "happy condition," were we thinking in terms of being totally "unconfined, unrestricted and unrestrained?" Certainly not!

Paul's New Testament concept of "freedom from the law" embraces three facets of liberty involving that law. *It first implies that Christ has liberated us from slavery to the ceremonial aspect of the law contained in ordinances and sacrifices.* When Jesus died on the cross, He fulfilled all that the ceremonial law represented. The former sacrifices and washings, so binding under Moses, are no longer necessary at all. Christ is now our sacrifice, and He washes us spiritually in His precious blood.

Secondly, it implies freedom involving the moral aspect of the law—the ethical and moral standard of righteousness which governs one's attitudes and actions toward God and man. We are free from the moral law so far as it involves the necessity of fulfilling its demands *as a means to salvation.* We are saved by faith through grace and not by any of our good works in fulfilling the moral requirements of the law.

On the other hand, does one who has been saved and Spirit-filled by faith through God's grace have no obligation at all to the moral law of God? Some would have us assume precisely that! But in that type of proposition, it does not necessitate a theologian to recognize that the outcome is not freedom, but rather unrestrained license! It is freedom totally abused!

So the third aspect of biblical freedom from the law is not freedom from performing the ethical and moral demands of the law. Rather, it is *soul freedom in the fulfilling* of such ethics and morality. I choose to call this MORAL SANCTIFICATION.

However, when we contemplate the relationship between experiencing soul freedom and fulfilling the moral law of God, we face the deeper, very intricate (inner) problem of selfishness and sin.

The problem is evident. Apart from cleansing grace, our inner sinful inclinations propel us in a direction contrary to the moral law's view of right and worthy performance. Now when one's conscience forbids what the inner propensities strongly desire, an inner collision of forces results. Such a clash of inner power, unless Christ intervenes by His Spirit, produces a type of bondage of another kind. The moral law which was designed for our good becomes "a yoke of slavery." Many perplexed and struggling persons have asked in desperation, "How can I be truly free and yet obliged to force myself into obeying what I, by nature, do not desire to obey?" I fully sympathize with the question! That is not freedom! That is the bondage of legality!

How then is biblical freedom found? Inner freedom results only when one's inner desires and moral obligations are harmonized! Inner freedom is an experiential reality only when one *loves* God's moral law! The heart of the psalmist was free as he triumphantly proclaimed, "O how I love Thy law! It is my meditation all the day" (Psalm 119:97).

Ah, yes! But how is such a heart full of love for God's moral standards obtained? If we find our inner desires propelling us in a direction contrary to such love, let us not ask our Lord to modify the commandments. Rather, let us ask Him to so cleanse our desires and purify our love by the infilling of the Holy Spirit that God's moral law will increasingly become our delight! The moral law of God will never set our hearts to music until our love for Him is so empowered by the Holy Spirit that it tends to propel us *toward* His standard of holy behavior.

When we allow the Holy Spirit to conform our inner drives and propensities to the holy demands of his moral law through Spirit cleansed love, the inner collision of forces is counteracted, and true biblical freedom results! As we maintain continual heart yieldedness to His will, the moral obligations of God's law of cease to be a galling yoke to our necks. We will be enabled by the Holy Spirit more and more to love His law. So then we are free! Within the gracious limits of the moral law of God we are free!

Father Faber experienced that freedom where many Protestants are missing it, and penned the following lines:
"And He hath breathed into my heart a special love for Thee;
A love to lose my will in His, and by that loss be free!"

Ah yes! Let us come to learn how free the sanctified can be!

WHAT OF THE PROCESS OF
CONTINUAL SANCTIFICATION?

Read: 1 Thessalonians 4:1-8

In our previous readings we have reflected on the sanctifying work of the Spirit from four standpoints: the Spirit's work which results in a sinner being "born of the Spirit" (INITIAL SANCTI-FICATION), Christ's work on the cross identifying us with Him in "being crucified with Christ" (PROVISIONAL SANCTIFICA-TION), the Spirit's work resulting in a Christian being "filled with the Spirit" (EFFECTUAL SANCTIFICATION), and the resulting "freedom of soul" in obeying the moral and ethical obligations to our God (MORAL SANCTIFICATION). Now consider with me the Spirit's ongoing work in the heart and life of the Christian which results in that person "growing in the Spirit." This involves CONTINUAL SANCTIFICATION, and is brought about through process and results in progress (1 Thessalonians 4:1-8).

One of the most spiritually devastating errors a Christian can make is to assume that unrealistic, more than biblically-warranted results will be forthcoming when his faith embraces the deeper cleansing of the infilling of the Holy Spirit. Such expectations will surely result in inner spiritual disappointment. For instance, to suppose that being filled with the Holy Spirit will make loving obedience to God a cinch is simply to expect too much—even though there will exist a sense of additional spiritual power! The presumption that such fullness will assure, in a computer-like way, nothing but victory—patient kindness and unruffled peace—is fool-ish and unreal. To expect an all-sufficient, one time blast and infusion of power that automatically ensures the recipient will never commit another sin is simply not biblical (1 John 2:1).

Sooner or later the person who espouses such high-powered expectations will come to a realization that not everything he presumed happened in his heart during that crisis moment actually did! He may even begin experiencing an unnecessary series of inner doubts that he ever, in fact, experienced such fullness. He may be tempted to renounce his profession. Or conversely, he might possibly be tempted to compromise his own intellectual honesty. How? By neatly sweeping under the snug rug of his profession all of the inconsistencies of his real inner experience which contradict that which he expected to happen in a crisis moment. He may choose to persist in that profession by tenaciously (and dishonestly) claiming more than he knows he possesses. Feelings of guilt will surely follow, and such feelings will torpedo true inner peace. Eventually growing disappointment and utter despair are guaranteed!

It is much more freeing to the conscience for the Spirit-filled Christian to honestly realize and accept the realities which are involved in sanctifying grace.

Though one may be full of the Holy Spirit, circumstances will surely enter his life which will force him to realize his recurring need for "extra fillings," as did the Spirit-filled disciples who prayed in Acts 4. Incidents calling for new and fresh power to choose to obey God whether one feels like it or not will often arise. New issues will challenge him, necessitating deeper consecrations and the updating of his full yieldedness to the Father. Unguarded harshness and displays of impatience will call for honest, penitent confession both to God and others. This will happen often enough to the very best among any of us to convince us that we have not yet attained final sanctification! Periodic and deeper cleansings will become necessary to keep the heart pure. All of this involves growth, development, improvement and progress in the continual reception of the ongoing work of the sanctifying Spirit!

We must understand one fact clearly. In the Christian life there is no state of grace this side of heaven which would warrant one to believe he needs no more of the improving work of the Spirit. The imperfections of the sanctified are many! The personalities of most Spirit-filled people are roughshod at best. It will take the better part of a lifetime for the Holy Spirit, through His ongoing sancti-fying activity, to mold and shape most of us into becoming as truly Christ-like as God really desires us to be. We must "keep on being filled with the Spirit"—or "ever be filled with the Spirit" (Ephesians 5:18). So let us keep on yielding to God! Let us pretend nothing! Let us not imagine "arrival"! Let no "spiritual" smugness of any kind creep over our demeanor! Let us truly recognize how far short we fall of His perfection! Let us persist in trusting nothing but the undeserved merits of the cleansing blood of Christ! Let us keep striving! This is CONTINUAL SANCTIFICATION! Our next conclusive reading on this subject will encourage us to antici-pate our FINAL SANCTIFICATION.

WHEN WILL SANCTIFICATION BE FINAL?

Read: 1 Corinthians 15:52-53; 1 John 3:1-3

When will sanctification be final? The answer to that question leads us to our consideration of the sixth and final aspect of the sanctifying work of the Spirit. In previous readings we have tried to understand more fully the first five aspects of this subject: INITIAL SANCTIFICATION, when one is "born of the Spirit"; POSITIONAL SANCTIFICATION, involving "crucifixion with Christ"; EFFECTUAL SANCTIFICATION, when a Christian is "filled with the Spirit"; MORAL SANCTIFICATION, involving inner soul freedom in obeying God's moral precepts; and CONTINUAL SANCTIFICATION as the child of God is "growing in the Spirit."

The sixth is FINAL SANCTIFICATION. Final sanctification involves that aspect of the Spirit's work which will result in "what one will finally be in the Spirit." It involves the culmination of all that is included in the entire scope of His great sanctifying work. It will be experientially realized in final glorification.

Some day, at a time known only to God, Jesus Christ will return to this earth a second time. Many of us refer to the first phase of His second coming as "the rapture" based on the description given in the Bible of the main incident which will take place at that time. The apostle Paul describes this event in 1 Thessalonians 4:16-17: "For the Lord Himself will come down from heaven with a loud command, with the voice of the archangel and with the trumpet call of God, and the dead in Christ will rise first. After that, we who are still alive and are left will be caught up (snatched away, raptured) together with them in the clouds to meet the Lord in the air. And so we will be with the Lord forever."

All who have died trusting Jesus Christ, and all who will be alive and living in faith when Christ returns in the rapture, will experience that transaction! This incident will include every believer of every age. All will be completely changed by a mighty work of God's grace—the final stage of His sanctifying work! This change will take place "in a flash, in the twinkling of an eye, at the last trumpet. For the trumpet will sound, the dead will be raised imperishable, and we (who are living) will be changed. For the perishable must clothe itself with the imperishable, and the mortal with immortality" (1 Cor. 15:52-53). We will, in that moment, receive glorified bodies made anew in the likeness of the glorified body of God's risen Son! We will "be like Him, for we shall see Him as He is" (1 John 3:1-3). Our bodies will be clothed with immortality and our minds perfected! Our spirits will be set completely free! At that point sanctification will be completed to its fullest degree! The culminating phase of the Spirit's sanctifying work will be experienced! What a glorious, all-embracing hope is ours!

This hope of the return of our Lord serves even now as our greatest motivating drive toward becoming partakers of His holiness through His present sanctifying work. John wrote, "But we know that when He appears we shall be like Him, for we shall see Him as He is. Everyone who has this hope in Him purifies himself, just as He is pure" (1 John 3:2-3).

What aspect of His sanctifying work do you need God's Spirit to work in your heart or every day living? Do you need to be born again? Is your need to reckon yourself to be dead indeed to sin? Do you need to be filled with the Spirit? Are you enjoying inner freedom of soul in your obedience to Him? We all certainly need the continual, progressive aspect of His sanctifying work, don't we? Someday, when Christ returns we will all partake in this final aspect of His all inclusive sanctifying work!

As you seek His effective work at the point of your inner heart need, be very encouraged, "because from the beginning God chose you to be saved through the sanctifying work of the Spirit and through belief in the truth. He called you to this through the gospel, that you might share in the glory of our Lord Jesus Christ" (2 Thessalonians 2:13-14). Even so, amen!

WORKING OUT OUR
CONSECRATION
AND HIS FULLNESS

"We are not satisfied with being faithful; we deeply desire the special awareness of God's blessing upon our faithfulness. We are not satisfied to work hard; we look to God for His empowering upon our earnest efforts. We seek for something more than busyness; we seek the evidence that God uses us."

Wesley L. Duewel
Taken from ABLAZE FOR GOD
By Wesley L. Duewel
Copyright © 1989 by Wesley L. Duewel
Used by permission of
Zondervan Publishing House

What are the Results of Total Commitment?
What is the Sequence of Power and Witnessing?
How Needful is His Fullness?
How Brightly Are You Burning?
What Are We to Do with "This Old Man"?
How Will the Spirit's Fullness Affect Our Worship?
Do You Need an Extra Filling?

WHAT ARE THE RESULTS OF TOTAL COMMITMENT?

Read: Romans 6:19; 12:1-2

Is it possible for one to be truly honest at gut level, and at the same time declare himself/herself to be totally committed to Jesus Christ? J. Wilbur Chapman met General William Booth, founder of the Salvation Army, when the General was past eighty years of age. The evangelist asked Booth to disclose to him something of his secret for success. The old warrior of many spiritual battles and victories hesitated a slight moment as tears welled up in his eyes. Then he spoke: "I will tell you the secret. God has had all there was of me. There have been men with greater opportunities; but from the day I got the poor of London on my heart, and a vision of what Jesus Christ could do with the poor of London, I made up my mind that God would have all of William Booth there was. And if there is anything of power in the Salvation Army today, it is because God has all the adoration of my heart, all the power of my will, and all the influence of my life." Dr. Chapman left that meeting with William Booth convinced "that the greatness of a man's power is the measure of his surrender."

I ask again, is such yieldedness really within the realm of possibility? With the fluffy type of commitment which is so much the order of our day, Booth's sincere response offered in a previous era will, without doubt, be dismissed by some "warmed over evangelicals" today as "stretched and spiritualized." Much more palatable to current taste would be a "pseudo-humble, all-inclusive confession" that "no one can be that committed to *anything* on an ongoing basis, let alone to God!" That fits contemporary shoe leather much more comfortably.

Ah! But does our flabby notion of the restricted extent of our God-given willpower, so broadly embraced today, alter at all the clear intent of the apostle Paul's statements in Romans 6:19 and 12:1-2? Of course not! "...Just as you used to offer the parts of your body in slavery to impurity and to ever increasing wickedness," exhorts Paul, "so now offer them in slavery to righteousness leading to holiness." Again, "I urge you, brothers, in view of God's mercy, to offer (present) your bodies as living sacrifices, holy and pleasing to God—which is your spiritual worship. Do not conform any longer to the pattern of this world, but be transformed by the renewing of your mind. Then you will be able to test and approve what God's will is—his good, pleasing and perfect will."

What are the results of total commitment? They are distinguished by at least four identifying characteristics. First, total commitment is MAKING A DEFINITE DECISION! This certainly includes any area calling for commitment—especially commitment to the Lord! It calls for a strong exercise of one's power to determine, to resolve, to come to decision! There can be no *original* commitment or *ongoing* commitment without decision.

Secondly, total commitment results in the REORGANIZING OF ONE'S PERSONAL PRIORITIES! "Strengthen the spirit—mortify the flesh!" "God's will at any cost!" "God first, others second and ourselves last!" "Be not satisfied with the good when the best is available!" These are moving sentences and phrases which call for prioritizing. But they do tend to sound more attainable on Sunday mornings than Thursday afternoons. Honestly reorganizing one's personal priorities is far from easy!

Thirdly, total commitment results in TAKING DIRECT ACTION! It demands that we actualize what we prioritize. This also is much easier to state than to fulfill, obviously. Most evangelicals find it more exciting to speak to each other of "carefully prioritizing the activities of our daily routines" than to actually do it! But doing it is what embodies the actual commitment!

Fourthly, total commitment calls for FOLLOWING THROUGH! Our attitude of commitment must become a resolve to commit. And such resolve must produce actions of commitment. Actions of commitment must develop into a life of commitment. The committed life—that is the goal!

I ask one final time, is it possible for one to be continually and totally committed to Christ? Most certainly it is! Is it easy? No—not at all! But let us be reminded of Paul's encouragement following his call to such commitment: "For sin shall not be your master, because you are not under the law, but *under grace*" (Romans 6:14). By His wonderful grace, let us be certain we are totally committed to our God!

WHAT IS THE SEQUENCE
OF POWER AND WITNESSING?

Read: Acts 1:8

The words of Jesus must have rung in the disciples' ears as they hurried back to Jerusalem from the scene of Christ's ascension to the Father! His promise had been two-fold and forthright: "I am going to send you what my Father has promised" (Luke 24:49a), and "you will receive power when the Holy Spirit comes on you" (Acts 1:8a). Likewise, His mandate was two-fold and clear: "Stay in the city until you have been clothed with power from on high" (Luke 24:49b), "and you will be my witnesses in Jerusalem, and in all Judea and Samaria, and to the ends of the earth" (Acts 1:8b).

It was absolutely imperative for the disciples to recognize the importance of the sequence represented in Jesus' statement. First, they needed to stay in the city of Jerusalem *until* they were clothed with power from on high. Only then would they be adequately enabled to set out to be His effective witnesses throughout their own land and to the ends of the earth!

How did they respond? They obeyed Jesus and returned to Jerusalem and "joined together constantly in prayer" (Acts 1:14). Certainly they did more than pray, but pray they did—constantly! On Pentecost Day it happened! They were all filled with the Holy Spirit, and they began to declare the wonders of God among the multitude gathered in the city. Whereas, Peter was the chief spokesperson, all of them—120 strong!—shared openly! No less than three thousand persons accepted their message and were baptized! These continued to meet in the temple courts every day praising

God, and the Lord added to their number daily those who were being saved. Obviously, history records the rest of the story.

Oh, that we could see in our day, as they did then, the very practical necessity of such a sequence for us. I am forced to grapple with my own serious doubts as to whether those words have truly gripped us today with the same intensity as they must have affected those early hearers. So very few seem to have come to terms with both prerequisites as well as the full scope of the mandate and the promise. Too often, we who today would be His faithful witnesses in our communities and cities throughout the U.S. and around the world, magnify the pressing necessity to win the lost, plant new churches, and go into all the world with the gospel. Rightly so! Ah yes! Rightly so!

But sadly, on the other hand, we also tend to minimize, by our lack of responsiveness, the equally pressing necessity to wait before God in constant, earnest prayer until we have been endued with the power of the Holy Spirit. How often we lose sight of the biblical and very obvious fact that truly effective witnesses must be Spirit-filled witnesses!

In my own denomination a number of years ago, we who were entrusted with district and denominational leadership met to try to discern just what the Holy Spirit was saying to us regarding our God-given obligation to fulfill Jesus' Great Commission. Knowing we must embrace the call of Jesus to be His witnesses in our own Jerusalems, Judeas and Samarias, and around the world, the ten district superintendents spent quality time with the president discussing the challenges of how to do our part in this great worldwide endeavor.

We took a good look at our core values, our vision and direction, our purpose statement and our goals and objectives. We concluded that for us, nothing would be more important, either in the U.S. or in missionary work overseas, than planting new churches and growing healthy churches! We have happily discovered that many other denominations share the same passion. We have purposed to do the work ourselves, as well as cooperate in every way we can, strategically, with other evangelical denominations to fulfill the Great Commission.

But we concluded, as have many other leaders of sister denominations across America who have seriously committed to this task, that there are two great steps of spiritual preparation which are absolutely necessary if we are to meet these challenges effectively: We must be a people committed to prayer, and we must become and remain filled with the Holy Spirit.

As it was with those early disciples, so it must be with us. We must be continual recipients of the fullness of His Spirit and power, and purpose to operate in His strength. Then we can be His effective witnesses, do the work of evangelism with confidence, win the lost, and aggressively plant growing, healthy churches in new areas across the U.S. and abroad. God help us to do so!

HOW NEEDFUL IS HIS FULLNESS?

Read: Acts 2:1-8

Often God's blessings slip upon us unannounced. I recall one such occasion while I was serving as a missionary in Nigeria, West Africa many years ago. I was teaching in the Salka Hausa Bible School in the north section of the country. For a week our class had discussed the work of the Holy Spirit. As the period was drawing to a close, I concluded with an illustration of the Spirit's work in purifying the heart of the Christian. I closed my Bible and put away my notes. Unexpectedly, one of the young men in the class stood to his feet to speak. "I know I have received this cleansing, but I feel I have allowed myself to drift. I do not sense God's presence as I once did. I want you to pray for me." Immediately an intensity of God's presence settled upon us.

As he was seated one of the other students stood. "I know I am a true Christian. My sins are forgiven," he said, and continued to give a glowing testimony of his conversion. "But," he went on, "I have never been able to fully and completely consecrate myself to God as we have heard taught in this course. I want to pray now that God will help me to give myself fully to Him. I want His purity."

As he sat down, another rose to request the same. Without any urging, a fourth rose to speak. I felt a welling sense of gratitude to the faithful Spirit as he expressed his need: "For a long time I have been thinking seriously about this work of the Holy Spirit. One time Mr. Boettger (another missionary working in the northern part of Nigeria at that time) spoke to me and explained to me how the Christian needs to be filled with the Spirit. Ever since then I have been thinking. Now the Spirit is showing me again my need and failure. I want this cleansing, too."

I was especially happy as the fifth student stood. He had expressed some of his deep feelings in other classes. He stated, "I know I am not full of the Holy Spirit. Now I understand, and I too, want you to pray for me that the Spirit will cleanse my heart and fill me."

Six of these fine men had stood requesting that we pray for them, so the class period turned into a prayer meeting! To hear these men, one after another, raise their voices to God in faith for the blessed fullness of the Sanctifier brought tears to my eyes and praise to my heart. I also poured out my heart together with them that God would meet the needs of each of those seekers in cleansing power.

As we prayed I felt that it would be good if I requested each of them to publicly tell what God had done for him! I was certain it would help to seal their faith. But before I could verbalize my request, spontaneously they stood to their feet again, one by one, to give God praise for filling their hearts. It was a blessed scene!

It was very evident to me at that time that the need was overwhelming for Spirit-filled, well-trained men—prepared in head and heart—to become pastors in the northern villages of the country of Nigeria. To help in this preparation, the Salka Bible School was dedicated to teaching these men and their wives the truths of the Bible and its related subjects, to providing practical student village work as well as pastoral work, and to giving personal counsel. Today the Salka Hausa Bible School is run completely by the Nigerian Church. All the teachers are nationals. The school is much larger than it was when the incident I relate here transpired. The training is being done in a thorough way. However, none of this will take the place of the initial preparation which those six men received in their hearts the last week of that course. Without the abiding fullness of the Spirit, all else is poor preparation indeed.

The years have obviously, come and gone. The six men have been involved for many years in their various stations in life. Other students now sit at the desks where they sat. They have the same need these men expressed. They too, must seek the Spirit's fullness! The former students all discovered, as the present day students also will, that an ongoing victorious life and ministry is realized only as they keep a continual attitude of submission to God. Their dependency on the Spirit will become increasingly evident. As they learn obedience to the recognized will of God, they will understand more and more that it is "not by might nor by power but by my Spirit," as the Lord has spoken.

HOW BRIGHTLY ARE YOU BURNING?

Read: John 5:31-35

Jesus uttered a very significant statement about John the Baptist in John 5:35, "He was a lamp that burned and gave light!"

The one church in a small midwest town caught fire. The village fire truck raced, screaming to the scene. A large crowd converged as firemen battled the blaze. The town pastor elbowed his way among the people endeavoring to calm and comfort some of the faithful, but shocked, members of the flock. Then, among the onlookers, the parson caught a glimpse of a man in the throng whom he knew only slightly, and who had never darkened the church door. He seemed genuinely concerned, however, as he watched the flames lick the stately building into oblivion. The pastor slipped to his side and, placing his arm around his shoulder said, "George, I've never seen you at church before, but I want to thank you sincerely for your interest." Obviously embarrassed, George responded, "Yeah, I'm sorry, Reverend. I've never been to your church. I know I should've come before this—but, after all, this is the first time I've seen your church on fire! I guess the fire really drew a crowd!"

Maybe George was on to more than he realized. I was converted to Christ shortly before my 16th birthday during revival services at the Osolo Missionary Church on the northeast side of Elkhart, Indiana. I recall during some of the services I attended following that crusade hearing the Christians sing songs I didn't fully understand. One was "I was saying 'yes' to Jesus when the fire fell." Another went like this: "'Tis burning in my soul! 'Tis burning in my soul! The fire of heavenly love is burning in my soul!" I came to understand later that these songs gave vent to a facet of biblical truth which, for them, expressed the difference between joyfully living out "a stretching, sharing type of Jesus love" and living a Christian life "grump style." They truly wanted to be lamps which "burned and gave light."

Too often, among so many of us who claim Christ's name the disappointing tendency to "warm ourselves at someone else's fire" becomes a flickering substitute for a personal burning heart. To sincerely appreciate hearing the news of what God is doing in someone else's life can indeed be very encouraging. But at some point, we must ask ourselves quite candidly, "What is God, in fact, doing in my life? Am I truly allowing the Holy Spirit to ignite the flame of God's love on the inner altar of my own heart? As John the Baptist was, am I a lamp that is burning and giving light?"

Do we want burning hearts? John the Baptist, in whose honor Jesus gave the testimonial recorded above, offered his own witness which sheds some light on the secret of such burning and giving of light: "I baptize you with water for repentance. But after me will come one who is more powerful than I...He will baptize you with the Holy Spirit and with fire" (Matt. 3:11).

You recall, when this promise of the Father given through John the baptizer, was fulfilled on the Day of Pentecost, the writer Luke described what happened in terms of spiritual fullness: "All of them were filled with the Holy Spirit..." (Acts 2:4). So the promise of their being baptized with the Spirit was fulfilled when they were filled with the Spirit. The Holy Spirit then is the Divine Source of that spiritual burning which kindles the bright flame of love for God on the inner altar of one's heart. So, do we want "burning" hearts? We must be filled with the Holy Spirit! To possess a burning heart without the fullness of the Holy Spirit is no more possible than having physical fire with no fuel. Not only so, but we must maintain this fullness. As we walk in the Spirit, we must continually keep on being filled with His presence day by day as Paul admonishes us in Ephesians 5:18!

The prayer expressed in an old hymn recognizes that daily need of God's ongoing fire in our hearts: "Fire of God, burn on in me; burn all the dross and sin away! Burn on! Burn on! Prepare me for the testing day!" As we hurry on toward His return, and that testing day, let us be very sure that we are spiritually "dressed, ready for service and (keeping) our lamps burning, like men waiting for their master to return..." (Luke 12:35, 36).

I personally respond very positively to the way Joseph Ramseyer, former president of the Missionary Church, used to wrap up this whole concept of our need to have burning hearts. In his unique way he would declare, "Absent of fire, nothing else counts! Possessing fire, nothing else really matters! Hell trembles when men kindle!" Ah yes! Who could express it better?

Here is the question again: How brightly are you burning?

WHAT ARE WE TO DO WITH "THIS OLD MAN"?

Read: Romans 6:6

The incident transpired in Nigeria, West Africa in 1966. The years have sped by so quickly, but the circumstances which placed an exclamation mark at the conclusion of what happened are still indelibly stamped on my memory.

We had concluded a theology class in the Salka Hausa Bible School. James Garba, one of the Bible School students, raised his hand to ask a question. We were studying a passage from Erich Sauer's book, THE TRIUMPH OF THE CRUCIFIED (quite a popular book at that time, and one translated into the Hausa language). We had considered the significance of the cross to the Christian individually. Our study led to a discussion regarding the meaning of the cross in relation to "our old man" (Romans 6:6). The phrase "our old man" was translated directly into the Hausa language from the King James Version of the Bible. The rendering given by the New American Standard Version, and later by the New International Version (which obviously, was not yet published) I believe is better, "our old self." It refers to "all that we formerly were, by nature and conduct."

James' question was very open: "Every time I hear teaching about 'our old man' I am troubled. In my heart I am bothered by this nature. If I could just reach down and pull him out by force, all would be well, but I can't. What are we to do with *this old man*?"

Ah! It was a fair question and deserved a direct answer! As I understood Paul's explanation at that time, I offered what I felt to be a fair and scriptural reply. I look back now, not so certain that it was as totally "without alloy" as I had hoped. But it was sincerely given, and the Holy Spirit relayed enough of the actual truth to openhearted students to prompt a positive response on their part.

However, if James should ask me the same question today, I would still say to him, "No, James, we cannot reach down inside ourselves and pull this old self out by force. It is not a 'thing' we can get hold of. Yes, earnest prayer will help. But even after we have begged God for help, this inner nature may rise again to challenge our desire to please Jesus!" James and his fellow classmates listened carefully.

I was convinced then, and am still firmly persuaded, that this problem was (and is) not confined to an African student in a Bible school in Nigerian society. It has plagued every society—and every person in those societies, besides Christ—throughout history! A few more than 1900 years ago the apostle Paul flung out the same question James Garba had asked: "What a wretched man I am! Who will rescue me from this body of death?" (Romans 7:24). Christians in every age have grappled with the same inquiry! Paul answers his own plea: "Thanks be to God—through Jesus Christ our Lord" (Romans 7:25). In chapter 8 then it is evident that "the law of the Spirit of life" had "set (him) free from the law of sin and death" (Romans 8:2).

Yes, indeed! But what precisely does such freedom involve? And how does it come to be a living reality in our hearts? That was the scope of James Garba's question.

No, we certainly cannot pull "our old man" out with our own hands! On the other hand, we *can* bring ourselves—all that we are by nature and conduct—to the cross of Christ and consent to be identified with Christ's crucifixion on that cross. What is provisionally ours in Romans 6:6, the Holy Spirit can make experientially ours in our hearts as we "count ourselves to be dead to sin, but alive to God in Jesus Christ" (Romans 6:11). "The body of sin" can be "rendered powerless" or "done away with" (NASB, NKJV), that we should no longer be slaves to sin...."

We need to be cautioned at this point. The crucifixion of "our old self" should not be viewed as automatically assuring us of unhindered progress from that moment on. To translate "katargeo"— which literally means "to make or render idle or useless," and which can be applied in many varying ways—with the word "destroyed" in this context as in KJV (implying total obliteration), is simply too strong! However, as we bring ourselves to the cross of Christ, all that we formerly were by nature and conduct can be done away with through the work of the Holy Spirit. But let us be reminded that such can only be effective on a continual basis so long as we maintain the habit of consenting to keep crucified with Christ. If not, "the bitter root"—or "the root of bitterness"—will raise its head and spring up and trouble and defile us again (Hebrews 12:15).

Two weeks following that particular class, James and five of his classmates prayed earnestly in faith and consented to begin what developed into the habit of being crucified with Christ. Have any of them ever been "troubled" with this "old man" again? I would presume they have found, as have the majority of Christ's followers, that continually maintaining an attitude of being totally and truly crucified with Christ is not always a lark. I do understand, however, that at least four of the six have followed through with their commitment and are serving Christ faithfully to this day. The other two I cannot answer for. To the blessed Lord be praise for the four!

HOW WILL THE SPIRIT'S FULLNESS AFFECT OUR WORSHIP?

Read: Psalm 95:1-7

Personal spiritual fullness, if genuine, results in lasting renewal. Spiritual renewal will, without a doubt, directly affect our individual worship. It will greatly influence our understanding as well as our expression of that worship. So two questions regarding our worship, as it is influenced by our personal appropriation of the Spirit's fullness, are very much in order:

1. What, in fact, is the scriptural definition of worship?

2. What constitutes the most meaningful expression of such worship?

The *meaning* of worship must emerge from the concept offered by the original writers of Scripture. The two Old Testament words rendered "worship" both embrace the idea of "bowing down or falling flat, prostrating oneself before another in an attitude and act of humble submissive reverence." The word in the New Testament used by far more often than any other also means, "to prostrate oneself in humble submissive reverence, to honor and adore." The second most often used word simply means "to revere and adore." A third carries the idea of "performing homage by ministering to, or doing the service of, the one worshipped," and is translated with both the words "worship" and "serve." The meanings of the remaining words offer nothing more of significance.

So let me venture a broad personal definition of Christian worship: "Christian worship is an attitude and/or action of reverent love and honor for, and humble submission to the triune God, resulting in committed service to Him and for His sake." Worship is "of the heart" first, then expressed in action.

What then constitutes the most meaningful *expression* of such worship? Is it the raising of our hands, or clapping, or the closing of our eyes while singing worship songs? Or is it the maintaining of a more reserved attitude while expressing our reverence? Does it involve the faithful use of hymn books? Or are overheads more appropriate? Or does it matter anyway? Should we stand? Kneel? Sit? Whatever form our expression takes, the essential is that it be manifested with honesty and freedom of soul. Personal spiritual revival invariably births fresh new joy. New joy incites natural spontaneity. Genuine spontaneity does not "check with others" before expressing itself. Why then, do we Christians tend to become nervous when there are some among us who desire to demonstrate adoration or service to Christ in a different manner from that to which we have become accustomed? Or why do we ourselves so often cramp our own natural responsiveness during worship? Doubtless, it has something to do with the personal security afforded in the well guarded comfort zones of our own carefully formed habits. Or it may involve the fear of "how others may react" toward any such "new" expressions by us. It might, obviously and quite simply, be because we are not revived. Is it necessary, after all, that every type of worship be communicated within the same set of expressional guidelines? Must all other Christians be cramped to only the style which assures my comfort? Can we not worship our Christ personally without attempting to intimidate or manipulate anyone else into or out of any style of expression that he or she prefers? Any expression displaying itself as "worship" which is either stilted by intimidation or propelled by a desire to gratify others' expectations is not the result of a heart touched by the Holy Spirit, nor is it pleasing to God!

But are we at this point really dealing with the primary issue involving worship anyway? Is whether we raise our hands or clap or remain solemn and staid, the final measure of proper expression? True worship, after all, is certainly *more* than lending our participation to certain expressive actions, whether designed to be majestic or joyful, serious or exciting, drab or fun!

Such expression, however performed, must be motivated by reverence, love and honor for the Savior, and result in humble submission and committed service on His behalf. Any and all such actions, if lacking these ingredients, whatever else they may represent, cannot constitute true biblical worship!

Beyond this, while spiritual worship may express itself in isolated segments of actions performed in particular settings, more importantly, it embodies the day by day discipline which develops into a lifetime practice of loving, honoring, submitting to and serving our Lord! Our whole lives must be lived out in service to Him as "lives of worship!" That is, in fact, permanent renewal! Paul wrote in Romans 12:1, "Therefore, I urge you brothers, in view of God's mercy, to offer your bodies as living sacrifices, holy and pleasing to God—which is your spiritual worship ('reasonable service,' KJ)." Out of hearts that have been renewed by the Holy Spirit, let us so worship Him!

DO YOU NEED AN EXTRA FILLING?

Read: Acts 4:23-31

The record of the Acts of the Apostles is the historical, factual report of the work of the Holy Spirit in a missionary movement in and through men who kept full of His presence. The overflowing ministry of these men is remarkable in its demonstration of supernatural power.

What was their source of buoyant victory? Most of us in our reply to such a question (however we may interpret Acts 2) would include, possibly among other facets, "the fullness of the Spirit received on the day of Pentecost."

Ah yes, but let us not dismiss the question quite so quickly and simply as though to say that the initial infilling of the Holy Spirit received on that particular day loaded them with a certain mysterious blast of power which lifted and carried them in unhindered fashion victoriously to the close of their earthly ministries!

We find no valid reason, scripturally or experientially, to assume that one such experience will so assure us of an automatic victory. One incident recorded in Acts will serve to illustrate the point. In chapter four we read how some of these very apostles who had been filled with the Holy Spirit on the day of Pentecost met again in a similar prayer meeting. Peter and John had faithfully witnessed to the resurrection power of Jesus Christ. God had used them in a miraculous healing. They were arrested, however, for preaching the resurrection through Christ and had been warned not to preach any more in that name. Then they had been released by the authorities.

We know at this point these followers of Jesus faced "decision time!" They knew full well that these authorities had sufficient clout to make good on their threats. They had, not many days previous to this, seen to it that Jesus Himself was crucified. Sensing their need for added courage and boldness, they gathered with the saints for prayer.

Now in this prayer meeting it is evident that they were not depending on what had happened to them some weeks previous in the upper room on the day of Pentecost. This was a new situation! The power received at Pentecost was not sufficient for now. It was blessedly sufficient then, but this present challenge brought with it a new need for fresh courage. The record says, "After they prayed, the place where they were meeting was shaken. And they were all filled with the Holy Spirit and spoke the word of God boldly" (Acts 4:31).

These disciples who were already full of the Spirit were filled again! They were brought anew under the complete control of the One Who had already given them His fullness! Here was an "extra filling." This added infilling was just what they needed for that particular crisis hour and, with fresh buoyancy, "they spoke the word of God boldly."

I suggest that here is one of the main reasons for the lack of a freshness of soul on the part of so many of God's servants in our day. Here is one reason the work of the Lord limps along. It is one major reason the home church is weak when power is needed for effective evangelism. Here is one reason for fruitless efforts.

Let us recognize that much of the time it is not the original filling that is lacking. It is the lack of any "extra fillings." As new challenges face us, we rest on the fact that we have already been filled, and do not recognize our need for new incomings of the Spirit's presence and power to grant fresh courage and updated strength. Some would even fear that to confess such a need in prayer is to belittle the original filling received when they consecrated themselves to God. Others assert if we are already full of the Spirit we can't become "fuller," not realizing that a healthy soul is an ever-enlarging soul needing *ever* to be filled anew and afresh. Besides, the Holy Spirit is not "material" necessitating physical space for Him to fill. He is *spirit*—and He operates in our spirits! He can as easily fill a heart where He already dwells with a greater measure of Himself as He could come into a world where He already dwelt with greater intensity as He did on the day of Pentecost. Lack of physical space is not His hindrance. Unyielded hearts are what hinders His fullness!

Christian brothers and sisters, let us not allow ourselves to rest on the fact that at some crisis moment in the past we sought and received the baptism with the Spirit. That indeed may have been a tremendous milestone in our pilgrimage. But it was only the beginning of fuller measures of His sanctifying grace that God wants to work into our lives as we face new unfolding circumstances. Let us not feel that since He filled our hearts at that initial moment we have no further need of being filled.

We simply cannot afford to delude ourselves into feeling that the power and courage of that hour is automatically sufficient for today. Let us not feel that the Spirit has somehow loaded us with a one time, heavyweight supply of all the power and courage we need for every situation we will ever face in life. Let us humbly open our hearts for a fresh filling today. If we refuse, let us not be surprised at the dryness that may steal over our hearts, and the certain sense of cramped vision which will result, without a doubt. Let us not be surprised at our own lack of spiritual buoyancy as we watch others move on in God's work with a spontaneity that draws others to Jesus!

We need these extra fillings! As Paul has constrained us in his letter to the Ephesians, let us "keep on being filled with the Spirit" (Ephesians 5:18, orig.).

LEARNING TO PRAY

"...the key to world evangelization, thus clearing the way for Christ's return, may be your prayer and mine. If the main delaying factor is lack of prayer, do not be surprised if God makes special provision for prayer to be more effective today than ever before."

Wesley L. Duewel
Taken from TOUCH THE WORLD
THROUGH PRAYER
By Wesley L. Duewel
Copyright © 1986 by Wesley L. Duewel
Used by permission
of Zondervan Publishing House

Are We Leaning to Pray?
Have You Checked Your Prayer Lines Lately?
Who is the Customs Agent in Heaven?
How Real Can Answered Prayer Be?
How Shall We Pray for Balanced Renewal?
Can Our Thanksgiving be
       Honest and Exuberant Simultaneously?

ARE WE LEARNING TO PRAY?

Read: Luke 11:1

Prayer and revival! Which is the cause and which is the effect? I believe it surely works both ways. There has never been lasting biblical renewal unless someone (or many) first wrestled with God in earnest believing prayer! On the other hand, where the process of true revival is discernible, meaningful prayer certainly becomes a priority! It becomes a tremendously effective cycle!

A concerned pastor asked a typical wide-eyed boy in his congregation, "Jamey, do you pray?"

"Sometimes I pray," responded Jamey, "but sometimes I just say my prayers."

Does sheer honesty compel you and me to identify more closely with Jamey's unrecognized predicament than is comfortable? I, for one, must confess that my own personal quest for revival includes a real pressing need for a renewed "grip on God" in effective prayer. I know how to say prayers. That is not my need. I say prayers nearly every morning—and often throughout each day. I believe God answers prayer, so neither would that be my concern. My growing heart-cry is rather, "O God, teach me how to be more genuinely *effective* in my prayer life."

I do not know what your concern might be at this point. For me, the issue has not been that God would teach me to pray more profoundly, or even help me to spend more time in prayer (although I am sure I lack here also). My bottom line concern is that my own heart attitude of faith and total confidence in God will become more genuine. I want it to be "without wax," so the Holy Spirit will be able, with far less hindrance from me, to relay and represent my prayers to the Heavenly Father. I desire that two results will become much more clearly evident in my prayer life: first, that I will be able to pray more consistently and more truly "in the actual will of God" and "in the Spirit;" and secondly, that the Heavenly Father will be able to maintain His own flawless character and at the same time grant more genuine, biblical answers to my prayers.

I believe it would do all of us much spiritual good to ask ourselves periodically, "When was the last time I know God truly, without question, answered a prayer for me that I earnestly offered to Him?" It might be surprising—even rather shocking—how long some Christians would find they have gone without any clear indication of answered prayer at all! It might be amazing how many daily procedures of some Christians would go unaltered if God simply went out of business!

A poll conducted a few years ago reported that the average born again, lay person in evangelical, Bible believing churches prayed about four minutes a day. The average evangelical Bible preacher at that time prayed seven minutes a day. I was delighted to read recently that the preachers' average had increased in the last few years to 15 minutes a day! The lay person's had remained essentially unchanged. Now I am not at all convinced that God holds a time clock on our prayers. On the other hand, notwithstanding the increase on the part of the clergy, if such a poll does represent the level of priority biblical Christians give to prayer, we are fooling ourselves to expect that deep, lasting biblical revival and renewal will be forthcoming!

The most meaningful prayer with which many of us ought to begin is the prayer of confession! Such a lack of prayer among us—though not publicly, blatantly observable—is nonetheless wickedness in the sight of God. Let us honestly confess this to

Him. Then let us consecrate ourselves to Him and pray for the fullness of the sanctifying Holy Spirit. Finally, let us pray, my friend, let us pray! May God grant that our praying will be truly "in the Spirit," and that we—and our part of the world—will be changed for the better as a result of such praying.

"Lord, teach us to pray!"

HAVE YOU CHECKED
YOUR PRAYER LINES LATELY?

Read: Psalm 81:11-14

In Mark 1, we read that very early in the morning Jesus went to a solitary place to pray. In Luke 5, we are told that He often withdrew to lonely places to pray. In Mark 6, He went to the hills to pray. Prayer in the life of Jesus meant personal, private dialogue with His Father; personal, private discipline for the sake of His Father; and personal, private devotion to His Father.

If Jesus Christ, the very eternal Son of the living God, needed such solitary and extended times of prayer in His life, how much more must you and I need these times? Let's ask ourselves how intact our prayer life really is. Most pastors would admit that it is far easier to preach a sermon series on prayer than to practice consistently effective prayer in their everyday lives. Most of us know that it is far easier to discuss prayer than to pray! I wonder how many of us honestly feel "strong" at this point? On the other hand, what a tremendous privilege our Heavenly Father affords us of engaging in the same wonderful ministry Jesus had, of cooperating with His Father in the affairs of men through prayer (Hebrews 5:7-10).

How can we best participate in the realities of such a privilege? By pushing the Almighty at our fast pace? By praying consistently "on the run?" By attempting to "hurry God" by our "quickie prayers?" Most of us seem to know what we *want* as a result of prayer, don't we? And we know how to get right at the business of outlining clearly to God what we feel He should do for us and others and what His timing should be. Imagining time to be at such a premium, I sometimes wonder if we are trying to learn how to "feel successful" at doing "a lot of praying" in a very big hurry. And we wonder why God doesn't seem to "keep up" with our packed full schedules.

An incident in the life of Isaac illustrates the *deliberateness* of God's faithfulness in answering prayer. Isaac took Rebekah as his wife when he was 40 years of age according to Genesis 25:20. We read in Genesis 25:21, "Isaac prayed to the Lord on behalf of his wife, because she was barren. The Lord answered his prayer, and his wife Rebekah became pregnant."

"The Lord answered his prayer!" That seems simple and speedy enough, doesn't it! But only when we read on through to verse 26 do we see when it was that God actually answered Isaac's prayer. Rebekah gave birth to twins, Jacob and Esau, when Isaac was 60 years of age! That apparently means Isaac prayed faithfully for 20 years! Only after 20 years of persistence did Isaac actually see his prayer answered! God fulfilled His promise, both to Isaac and to his father Abraham—but only in His own timing.

In our day of instant pleasure, fast-foods and speedy computers, I wonder what this type of response does to us? I am convinced we are prone to give up far too soon and to doubt God's interest in answering our prayers because we are tuned in so unflinchingly to our twentieth century time clocks! God is not hemmed in by our 60 second stopwatches and 30/31 day calendars! God answers prayer, but always by His own timepiece.

I wonder if many among us have yet to learn how to really patiently "wait before God" in silent expectancy, listening carefully for His own direction in our praying (Ps. 81:11-14). What would happen if we would take time to truly die to our own imaginations and those desires for what we so strongly feel we want to pray, and then in simple trust ask God for His clear direction in our praying? Let's acknowledge that we cannot really pray effectively without the direction and energy of the Holy Spirit (Romans 8:26). We need to ask God to completely control us by His Spirit and in complete submission to Him, accept by faith that He does (Ephesians 5:18). In that submission, let us give the Holy Spirit the time and freedom to convict us, should there be any unconfessed sin. Let us take the necessary time to be sure our hearts are clean in the sight of God (Ps. 139:23-24).

Then let us ask God to teach us how to deal very aggressively with the enemy—to come directly against him in the all-powerful name of Jesus (James 4:7)! With praise to God and in unwavering faith, let us fully expect our God to do something very consistent with His character—both for us and through us, and for others for whom we pray.

Call it legalism or call it a spiritual principle, the old saying is invariably true: "Much prayer—much power! Little prayer—little power! No prayer—no power!" Most of us have found by both sad and ecstatic experience, that is just the way it works! I pray the Lord will help us to understand that fact. And let us pray!

WHO IS THE CUSTOMS AGENT IN HEAVEN?

Read: Hebrews 9:23-24

On what basis do we enter the holy presence of our Heavenly Father—whether to pray or to simply live in relationship with Him? Our stock answer obviously is, "We enter through Jesus Christ." Ah, yes—but what precisely do we mean by such a normally accepted response?

In 1987 my wife, Retha, and I visited our World Partners missionaries in Spain. Our first stop on the journey landed us in Madrid where a longtime friend, with whom we had worked as missionaries in Nigeria, met us at the airport. Rev. Jacob Bawa had been the principal of the Salka Hausa Bible School where we taught, and was the former president of the Missionary Church in Nigeria. He was at the time of our Madrid landing, the Nigerian ambassador to Spain and to the Vatican.

Following a time of joyous greeting and excited conversation, Mr. Bawa picked up a couple of our bags and signaled for us to follow him past the customs agents. I hesitated momentarily. "Mallam Jacob," I protested rather innocently, "we need to pass through customs first." Moving past me as he betrayed a rather half teasing, but very genuine smile, he whispered loudly enough so that Retha could also hear, "I am the ambassador! We are immune. Just follow me."

I looked at my wife with a questioning shrug but decided, "Why not?" We picked up our remaining luggage and followed him. As we approached the guards, I nodded hesitantly as Retha and I followed Jacob closely. As Jacob displayed his ambassador's insignia we walked right past their obliging expressions of approval, and entered Spain fully accepted!

Now let it be fully understood that Retha and I did not enter Spain because the authorities knew who we were. But they *did* know who Jacob was! The fact that we were American church leaders did not impress those guards at all. The fact that Jacob was the ambassador did! Our worthiness or lack thereof meant nothing to them. It was the ambassador's name and that he was worthy which allowed us to enter their country. He became our representative. They fully accepted Jacob Bawa. And in him, they accepted us. Retha and I entered Spain through the merit of his person, his position and his name alone!

Let us be extremely careful never to carelessly disregard this fact, spiritually. It is only through the person, position and name of our Lord Jesus Christ that we can truly pray and live in the presence of our great God of holiness. Following His death on the cross and His powerful resurrection, the Hebrew writer states that, in the heavenlies, Christ "entered the Most Holy Place once for all by His own blood" (Hebrews 9:12). He further asserts, "He entered heaven itself, now to appear for us in God's presence" (Hebrews 9:24). The Heavenly Father accepted His Son as our substitute—and in Him He has accepted us! We may now follow Christ into the very presence of the Father. It is not through our own righteousness, however, that we enter. It is through His! It is not our worthiness nor lack thereof, that impresses the Father. It is the holiness of His Son that demands His attention! Our own sacrifice or consecration is not what has touched the Father's heart to allow us to follow His Son. It is the sacrifice of Jesus Himself that has opened the way! So now we do not go hesitantly and with a questioning shrug as Retha and I did following Ambassador Bawa into Spain, but "with a sincere heart in full assurance of faith" (Hebrews 10:22).

Yes, thank God, the way is now wide open, and we are fully

accepted into the presence of our holy Heavenly Father! First, having fully accepted our divine representative, the Father also has accepted us in Him! We have entered and live in the presence of His holiness through the merit of His person, His position and His name alone! To Him and to Him alone, be glory forever and ever! Amen!

HOW REAL CAN ANSWERED PRAYER BE?

Read: Isaiah 58:5-9

The words of Isaiah are simple, but strong:

"Then you will call, and the Lord will answer; you will cry for help, and He will say, 'Here am I'" (Isaiah 58:9).

Just how real can answered prayer be? Two of my very special friends of the last more than 25 years live in Marshall, Michigan. Bob and Veda Anderson, now members of the Battle Creek Missionary Church, and in their late, young seventies, maintain that God always answers prayer! When pressed for complete honesty, Veda's quick response is, "Yes, He always answers. Sometimes 'yes,' and sometimes 'no,' but He always answers!"

"Sometimes He does it in such a wonderful way," she shared with me one day, "that we are absolutely astounded! I must tell you of an instance that I shall never forget." She related that one night Bob gave her $150 extra to plan for groceries that month for they were anticipating a big end-of-the-month dinner with their children and their families ($150 was no small amount for them!) However, a couple of weeks into the month, a persisting heart condition required Veda to enter the local hospital. In preparing to leave for the hospital she discovered that the $150 was not in her billfold where she thought she had placed it. Following a rather frantic, but futile, search of every little hiding place in the house, she and Bob reluctantly departed to admit her to the hospital. The visit from Bob and the rest of the family that first night brought her cheer. But her concern for the lost money would not allow her to relax. Where, after these weeks, could that money be?

Upon her family's departure from the hospital room, Veda prepared for her evening prayer and some sleep. Thanking God for her wonderful family, she prayed, "Lord, only you know what happened to that money. You know how desperately we need it. So please, either tell Bob where it is, or show me." She repeated her prayer a second time. And suddenly (with her eyes still closed) this friend of mine, who is not given to radical and strange experiences, "saw a big picture of their large garbage can with a bright light shining on it." She opened her eyes, astonished! "When I closed my eyes again," she explained, still with a touch of amazement in her voice, "the picture was still there!" Wondering just how real, or unreal, this rather bewildering experience might be she prayed, "Lord, what are you trying to tell me?"

Anticipating by now that I might be feeling the beginnings of skepticism—though she knew I fully believed in her integrity— she continued, "Then the garbage bags in the large can appeared, the big black ones for outside trash, and the little white ones for the kitchen. And, to my amazement, there in one of those white bags about eight inches from the bottom was a wad of green money!" Thanking the Lord Jesus, she picked up the phone and called her surprised husband. "Then," Veda said, "once more I closed my eyes thanking and praising Jesus for that wonderful answer to prayer and the great method He used to do it."

Bob never told me how he really felt as he listened to the story from his otherwise very normal wife. Nor did he tell me what he thought some of his neighbors might be wondering as they saw him sifting through those white trash bags. What he did say, he said to Veda: "You pray for me—and I will search every bag until I find it." And search he did! You guessed it—he found the money—about eight inches from the bottom in one of those white trash bags!

By morning nearly every nurse in the hospital had heard the news! When Bob arrived with the money in his hand, he simply stated, "It was right where Jesus said it was." Two of the nurses responded, "This is enough proof for us! We're going to let Jesus change our lives!"

"I sure hope they did," Veda expressed to me, then concluded her testimony with a couple of questions and answers of her own: "How did we lose the money? The only answer we have is that I put it on the table and forgot to take care of it and it got entangled with other papers and thrown away." Then, with a twinkle in her eye, "How did we find the money? A miracle!"

My personal heart conviction is that her assessment is right on target! What do you think?

Oh yes! Veda did come out of the hospital feeling much better in two or three days—and the end-of-the-month family meal was a grand time for all. They all marvelled at how God had made that meal possible.

HOW SHALL WE PRAY FOR BALANCED RENEWAL?

Read: James 4:7-10

"Submit therefore to God," says James in chapter 4 of his epistle. "Resist the devil and he will flee from you. Draw near to God and He will draw near to you." Are you and I deeply bent on "drawing near to God?" Let us ask ourselves sincerely, "Precisely what, of necessity, will clearly mark our personal walk with Jesus if we truly follow a biblical path toward spiritual renewal?" At that point, depending upon the depth of heart sincerity, two extremes could strongly beckon for the response of both of us —one overly negative, the other ultra positive. The first would demand us to focus only and totally on finding out what is "wrong" involving our relationship with God. The other will shove us in the direction of "not being concerned at all about what is wrong" but rather with the sole issue of "what God makes right." It is my conviction that neither, when followed alone, will result in bona fide renewal!

I intentionally choose not to be identified with those who are convinced that, in order to come to genuine renewal in Christ, we must become persistent pietistic sleuths committed to perpetual spiritual introspection. One of course, through a perfectionist's set of spiritual glasses, may be given to nothing except a nonstop type of ruthless self-examination of the maze of complicated attitudes and unpolished personal motives everyone of us periodically experiences. If so, he will invariably find enough unsatisfactory material to result in a rather predictably consistent state of depression. This will be true, no matter how full of the Holy Spirit he may be or how much biblical renewal is desired. Personal abiding revival will surely be elusive no matter how sincerely he prays!

On the other hand, the one who courts an abnormally inflated image of God's grace will probably follow the other path devoutly ignoring the glare of any inner sinfulness in the heart. He will develop a rather smug mindset toward the necessity of any type of moral auditing of his inner intentions or outward actions. He will likely tend to cover his inconsistencies in a snug fashion with his artificial definitions of both "sin" and "free grace"—and find himself empty—no matter how much he prays!

Do you and I really want to draw near to God? We must somehow strike a healthy spiritual balance between these two extremes. Such balance will include both the development of an honest introspective frame of mind, as well as a positive and sensible attitude of confidence toward God's keeping and renewing grace. Healthy introspection, rather than being unrelentingly and destructively perpetual, needs to be periodic and well-timed to actual inner needs. It must, however, be deeply honest, scripturally based, led by the Spirit, and open to recognize and accept the reality of any inner sin. Rigid resistance to the devil's temptation to hedge must be intentional! Sins cannot be dismissed as harmless mistakes! Any spiritual carelessness must be clearly confronted. Prayerlessness dare not be excused. Carnal attitudes must be recognized and confessed honestly. Such confession to God must be complete and sincere. Any necessary confession to a brother or sister, accompanied by a sincere request for forgiveness, needs to be thorough and absent of any whining. No excuses! No arguing with God or man! Just simple confession!

Then this straightforward attitude of confession on our part, must be coupled with a simple, but tenacious faith which fully accepts that God in free mercy does, in fact, receive such contrition. Let this faith embrace the fact that, through the indwelling work of the Holy Spirit made possible by the shed blood of Jesus Christ alone, all is "covered and cleansed and made right!"

Then let us thank Him for His mercy and let the genuine praises begin! Let the joy of the Lord once again become our strength! Worship His holiness! Let us bless His name and recognize our blood bought right to be glad! Let careful and loving obedience to God and His word through the Spirit's inner power, become the continual outflow of our lives! Let continual heart submission to His known will become the norm. This, I believe, is the beginning of personal balanced renewal. Oh God, grant all of us the grace to so draw near to you!

CAN OUR THANKSGIVING BE
HONEST AND EXUBERANT SIMULTANEOUSLY?

Read: Psalm 100:1-5

The Psalmist has urged us who have been "saved from distress" and "rescued from the grave" to "sacrifice thank offerings and tell of His works with songs of joy" (Psalm 107:22). True believers in Jesus ought to be the most thankful people in the world! We ought to give clear verbal expression to our thanksgiving often—and publicly! Such thanksgiving to God is positive and good! Thanksgiving with joy is better!

Christians who may be endowed with my "matter-of-fact" type of personality can create unnecessary problems for themselves when they endeavor to respond to this clearly beneficial injunction. "The honest facts" are very important to us when we listen to any type of praise or thanksgiving expression. In fact, we can tend to be so concerned with "factual integrity" in our own "bottom line" oriented type of worship, that even our heartfelt offerings of thanksgiving to God may not actually express much joy. They may have little moving effect on those who would be thankful with us.

Our kind of person is probably, too often, so intent upon the honesty with which the facts of one's thanksgivings are expressed that we tend to ignore the feelings with which such expression is given. You see, to us the integrity with which one's thanksgiving is voiced is every bit as important as the fact that thanksgiving has been given. Our obsession is not entirely without valid reason, of course! One of my own very personal gripes with some otherwise very respectable Christians is the tendency at times to slightly embellish and distort the content of joyfully expressed thanksgiving just enough so as to "make it a bit more exciting to hear." True, it will have a more moving effect on those who already sincerely desire to be thankful with them. But the hard cold fact is, such expression is not honest! People who are not knowledgeable of the facts may be impressed at hearing such thanksgiving—God won't! He says through the proverb writer, "A truthful witness gives honest testimony" (Proverbs 12:17), and the Lord "delights in men who are truthful" (Proverbs 12:22). The argument of Paul in Romans 4:5-8 would also certainly apply to such false expressions of "thanksgiving."

But stating my personal gripe does not solve my own problem. The problem Christians with my personality face is different, but can be just as stifling to any attempt to effectively express thanksgiving with genuine spiritual joy. A strong mindset bent toward "the cold hard facts" involved in expressing praise to God can, of course, mitigate against any type of free, natural response. Integrity's inclination is not to feel free to express what is not genuinely felt. By the time one completes his or her thorough and careful examination of "honest inner feelings" at every juncture of worship, however, the expression of such has become so mechanical that neither he nor anyone else cares!

At this point I am forced to ask myself, "Must feeling always be the indicator of genuineness in our expression of honest praise to God? Or is the issue the *fact* that our God *deserves* our thanksgiving and praise?" If it is the latter, then I ask further, "No matter how I may feel, should honestly expressed thanksgiving ever be dull? Is strict, closely guarded integrity designed to strangle the vibrancy of uninhibited joy out of sincere thanksgiving?" Cannot such integrity rather set a spiritual fire to that joy, and result in a conflagration of buoyant praise? Are we to assume that praise and thanksgiving which are offered "in a fitting and orderly way" (1 Corinthians 14:40) will always be expressed in a subdued and quiet fashion? I think not! Whatever else praise may be, it is honest thanksgiving offered to God with a live touch of exuberance!

Dear Brother Joe Sabo, Sr., a former pastor in my denomination, was a genuinely committed and happy saint of God. It was to my own personal benefit that I was privileged to know him and count him as a friend who regularly prayed for me! His long life of holiness and service in the work of Christ openly betrayed his love for His Lord. A few short years ago he passed into the presence of Jesus. He had learned long ago that praising God reverently, "in a fitting and orderly way," need not necessitate one's being overly subdued in such exercise. When people used to tell him that heaven would be a place of reverential quietness, he was known to respond, "I don't believe that. But if it is quiet in heaven, it won't be when I get there!" He praised God with open exuberance while he lived and I am quite sure that his praise could be heard throughout a good portion of the heavenlies when the angels welcomed him home!

Let's take Joe's example! Let's offer our thanksgiving to God with exuberance!

WORKING THROUGH CHANGE

"There is no power on earth that can neutralize
the influence of a high, simple and useful life."

Booker T. Washington
Taken from READERS DIGEST

How Do You Deal With Guilt?
What is Changing in Your Life?
Are We Affected or Effective Change Agents?
Will We Confront the Issues Involving Change?
Shall We be Contemporary or Traditional?
Are You Embracing "THE AGE WAVE" Change?

HOW DO YOU DEAL WITH GUILT?

Read: Romans 3:19-24

Paul writes, "For all have sinned and fall short of the glory of God" (Romans 3:23). Sin always results in personal guilt, and we must deal with personal guilt from two standpoints. There is first, the inner "feeling of guilt." There is secondly, the settled "fact of guilt." We are so prone to be obsessed with the *feelings* involving guilt because they affect our emotional responses and become, at times, extremely apparent in our conscious and unconscious reactions. However, our greatest issue of concern ought not be how we do or do not "feel" on the inside, but rather how we "stand" before the law of God! Our "standing" involves facts no matter how we *feel*!

On that count, the court of heaven has already heard our case. The verdict is already in. Every mouth is stopped and all the world has been rendered guilty before God and accountable to Him (Romans 3:19). We are "found" guilty before God—whether we *feel* guilty or not!

Certain members of our society have been greatly involved for the past number of years in a well orchestrated attempt to help us shed our inner "feelings of guilt." Their apparent failure, however, has been with the lack of any intent to motivate us to confront clearly the "fact of guilt." The church itself has inherited some of the residue of such efforts. Sermons are given, books written and counsel offered in a deliberate drive to help people rid themselves of their *feelings* of guilt toward themselves without ever dealing with the *fact* of their guilt before God! Such procedures simply cannot work! Our attitude toward guilt must change!

A classic illustration of this occurred in my ministry while I was in the pastorate. A troubled lady from outside the congregation was referred to me. "I have a real problem," she began. "I am divorced. I have a boyfriend. Sometimes he stays at my house overnight. On some of these occasions we have sexual relations." Then her announcement: "Now I want to tell you my problem." (I thought we had already gotten to her problem!) "My problem," she continued, "is that every time this happens, the next day my boyfriend feels so guilty! I just can't handle these unstable feelings of his! Please, can you help me to help him not to feel so guilty when this happens?" I suppose the blank look on my face signaled my confusion. I thought I had missed something! I asked her to repeat her problem. She did.

My response obviously, was not what she expected. "Of course he feels guilty!" I said, "He *is* guilty! I am surprised that *you* do not feel the same, for you are guilty, too!" (Tremendous counseling technique!)

Her eyes widened, she stiffened and said, "Well—I want you to know that I talked to another pastor (she named him) and he didn't tell me that." I knew the other pastor—and I knew quite well how he would have counseled her! It became apparent to me that she did not truly want help for her real problem. She had set out on a pastor-visiting excursion in a desperate attempt to find one among us somewhere who would be willing to help her and her boyfriend rid themselves of the "feelings of guilt" without every confronting the "fact of their guilt" before a holy God. What an exercise in futility! Their feelings didn't need to be pacified! Their hearts needed to be radically changed!

A young man who attended the church where I pastored asked me, "What subject do you plan to deal with next Sunday?"

"Why do you ask?" I inquired.

"Oh, I just wondered whether or not I could identify with your subject."

"I think you will identify quite well," I said with a knowing smile—I knew him well. "I am going to preach on the subject of 'guilt.'"

"Oh!—Well," he responded, "I didn't mean you had to preach on anything I could identify with that well!" At least he was honest! Then, only half sincerely, he asked what many others would like to ask: "Can't you preach a sermon once in awhile that will make guys like me feel good even if we know we are guilty?" Ah, there is the issue!

How are we to deal with our guilt? The Bible outlines one path. We must confront our sins squarely and face "the fact of our guilt" before God no matter how we "feel!" We must openly and honestly confess to God the sins which have caused such guilt. By His help we must turn away from those sins to Jesus Christ, and by faith lay all our guilt on Him. We must trust Him fully and completely for His full forgiveness. Only then will the words of the gospel song begin to ring with validity in our hearts: "Guilt is gone! Peace is mine, peace like to a river! Jesus is wonderful, mighty to deliver!" His deliverance and forgiveness formulate the only lasting answer to our problem of sin and guilt. The sooner we truly recognize this fact, the more quickly—and more thoroughly—our guilt problems will be genuinely solved on a long term basis! Let's respond accordingly!

WHAT IS CHANGING IN YOUR LIFE?

Read: 2 Corinthians 3:18

Most of us have come to some type of terms with *who we are* in Christ Jesus. A quick evaluation of our daily *performance*, on the other hand, might result in mixed feelings. Whether such a review brings total satisfaction or a mixture of pleasure and disappointment, I suppose we must consent to submit to Omar Khayyan's assessment: "The moving finger writes, and having writ moves on; nor all (our) piety nor wit shall lure it back to cancel half a line, nor all (our) tears wash out a word of it."

Has there been failure? Thank God we may confess such to Christ sincerely and accept His forgiveness humbly. Has there been success? We are duty bound to give Him all the glory! I urge that we take the admonition of Paul very personally, to "forget what is behind and strain toward what is ahead" and "press on" with full confidence in our Lord Jesus Christ (Philippians 3:12-14).

I want to offer three thoughts which embrace your future and mine, including all the potential changes for good or ill which loom on the horizon of those prospective days.

First, some things about our future are uncertain—they might change.

The tenacious hope that any changes which may occur in our lives will be positive tends to brighten our outlook! On the other hand, the distinct possibility that some changing circumstances could bring negative results tends to make the very best of God's people ill-at-ease at times. The psalmist wrote, "But I trust in you, O Lord. I say, 'You are my God.' My times are in your hands" (Psalm 31:15).

Forced job changes. Loss of one's home. Deteriorating health. Death of a loved one or friend. Financial set-backs. Dissipation of personal hopes and dreams. Divorce. Unrepentance of a son or daughter. Any of these changing circumstances and many others, could result in temporary or permanent reversal and threaten to radically alter our prospects for a bright future in a negative way. Our hopes, of course, are positive. But some things are uncertain. They might change. So we need to be forcefully reminded that "our times are in His hands!" We must totally trust all of our future to Him who "in all things works for the good of those who love Him, who are called according to His purpose" (Romans 8:28).

Secondly, some things about our future are unfinished—they must change!

All of us need spiritual growth. God is not finished with any of us yet! Someone commented to a 90 year-old man, "You must have seen many changes in your lifetime," to which he replied, "Yes, and I've been against every one of them!"

One of the greatest hindrances to spiritual progress is our overwhelming desire to remain contentedly safe in and fitted for the religious ruts we now enjoy! Ruts offer security, comfort, predictability, persistence in the status quo. It is much more peaceful to continue as we are than to launch out in intentional change for the better. Shortcomings are much more tolerable under such circumstances and lack of growth acceptable. But God knows that, among the very best examples of His grace, there can be found enough that does not really enhance the image of Jesus to motivate a rather concentrated and continual course designed for marked improvement! No wonder Paul wrote, "And we who with unveiled faces all reflect the Lord's glory, are being transformed (changed!) into

His likeness with ever increasing glory, which comes from the Lord, who is the Spirit" (2 Corinthians 3:18). Oh, how true! Some things in our lives are unfinished. They absolutely must change!

Thirdly, some things about our future are unfailing — they never change!

It is reassuring that, in the midst of all the vacillating and wavering circumstances of life, our triune God never changes (Hebrews 13:8)! It is totally impossible for Him to be changed at all for the better, for He is already *absolutely perfect*! Nothing *exists* to which He may change which would make Him better! And for Him to diminish His character one iota would result in His being that much less than God! He cannot change at all and remain God! He is immutable, eternally constant (James 1:17)! He said of Himself, "I the Lord do not change" (Malachi 3:6).

Just as reassuring is the fact that the message of God's Word regarding His Son will not change! What comprises that message? It involves His virgin birth, His sinless life, His death on the cross for our sins, His mighty resurrection, His offer of salvation, His promise of the Spirit's fullness, His promise to build His Church, His promise to return to this earth, and His promise to take His own to heaven eternal. Ah yes, some things are unfailing. They never change!

In a changing world we serve a changeless Savior who wants all of our changing to make us more like Him! By His grace, let's be at it!

ARE WE AFFECTED OR EFFECTIVE CHANGE AGENTS?

Read: Matthew 5:13-16

This decade, as predicted by so many religious leaders, has proven to be pivotal in the history of the church and our nation. We have seen thrust upon us an avalanche of radical attitudinal changes which have resulted in tremendous pressures on our society. We are feeling these pressures in the areas of religion and morality. They continue to erupt in our social debates and in discussions in the field of education and are, more and more, rocking the medical world! They increasingly challenge the formerly accepted ethical measuring rods of business and baffle us in the court of law.

Mind you, some of these pressures have enforced lasting good! However, my deep concern is that many other of these battles for the mind have been aimed directly at undermining the very foundational values which our country, influenced by the church, has traditionally held since its founding to be morally, ethically and religiously right. We need only to take note of the dramatic public change of attitude in this last brief generation toward such issues as life-time marriage, child-rearing, homosexuality, abortion, authority and integrity. In a relatively recent report by the Cox News Service, Bob Dart asserts that only thirteen percent of the nation's people still believe in all ten of the biblical commandments and that nine out of ten citizens lie regularly. He reports that, for ten million dollars, seven percent of the people say they would kill a stranger—which ought to help spark the sale of high blood pressure medicine! The following note was received by the IRS a few years ago: "Gentlemen, enclosed you will find a check for $150. I cheated on my income tax last year and have not been able to sleep ever since. If I still have trouble sleeping I will send you the rest. Sincerely..."

Ah, yes, radical changes come! Moreover, in one way or another, we too, are making our contribution to bringing about some aspects of these changes. The bottom line question we must ask ourselves still has to be the one articulated by George Barna a few years ago in his stimulating book, THE FROG IN THE KETTLE: "Will we be effective change agents? Or will we be affected changed agents?" That is yet the question which must dig our consciences, dominate our evaluating processes, and drive us to deliberately fulfill our divinely determined duty!

What about the church in all of this? After all is argued, we must honestly confess that the pressure of negative societal changes have most certainly had their effect here, too! Here is one reason why we, by all means, must truly turn to God for a deep and abiding revival. We have not always been the effective change agents we could and should have been. We have at times, in fact, been *affected change* agents. Whereas evangelical Christians generally possess orthodox beliefs about God, Christ, Satan and the Bible, most of us know that the outer (and sometimes inner) momentum is against a careful integrating of our spiritual principles with our practical performances. Our high ideals don't always fit our shoe leather very comfortably. We are so often given to skin deep commitment and sloppy obedience. How subtly our original ideals of evangelistic missionary fervor at home and abroad can all but fade. Almost unconsciously we can slip quietly, and quite respectfully, into the self-fulfillment of ego fulfillment. And, it all can happen without a serious thought of giving ourselves in deliberate, willing, sacrificial service for the sake of Christ and others. This absolutely must change!

What must take place among us if we are to be authentic, *effective* change agents for good? I suggest five things. First, we must be filled with the Holy Spirit. Secondly, we must be very certain that the principles of the Scriptures do, in fact, formulate the solid groundwork for our beliefs and values. Thirdly, we must carefully live out those beliefs and values in our day-by-day lifestyle by continual dependence on the power of the indwelling Holy Spirit. Fourthly, we must decide clearly to give ourselves, first and foremost, in committed service to Christ on behalf of others in whatever profession we may be led to undertake. Fifthly, we must remember unmistakably, in every labor, that it is *not by might, nor by power, but by His Spirit* that success is realized. Let's get on with being *effective* change agents!

WILL WE CONFRONT
THE ISSUES INVOLVING CHANGE?

Read: Acts 10:1-23

It seems to me one of the greatest hindrances to lasting renewal in the church is unwillingness on the part of God's people (especially those of us in leadership) to really allow the Holy Spirit to work enough change in us to make us genuinely useful. We who speak to each other the most convincingly about our desire to see the church radically changed for the better are usually the most difficult for God to convince to change *anything*! Let's admit it to each other—and to God—it is difficult to change! We have developed our own set of strong feelings about what God likes and doesn't like. We have, quite conclusively, decided how He does and doesn't want to do things. Some of those conclusions are very stubbornly settled! Sometimes the most challenging work God must do is to shake up those tenacious feelings.

It happened to Peter (Acts 10:11). There simply cannot be any staunch opinions you and I espouse today which are nearly as strong as those Peter embraced concerning what must be necessary for Gentiles who desired to become believers in Jesus! They must begin to observe certain days considered by Jews to be "holy days" and abstain from certain "unclean foods"—and circumcision was an absolute necessity!

It took nothing less than a direct vision from God to shake Peter loose from those tough sentiments! Following a vision given to a devout, God-fearing Gentile in Caesarea named Cornelius, the Lord visited Peter in Joppa. In a trance Peter saw a large sheet let down from heaven containing all kinds of four-footed animals, reptiles and birds. Then the shocker! A voice commanded, "Get up, Peter. Kill and eat."

Holding the unrelenting feelings he did regarding "unclean foods," Peter responded as we might expect: "Surely not, Lord! I have never eaten anything impure or unclean!"

The voice of the Lord replied to this strong-minded, but misinformed follower of His, "Do not call anything impure that God has made clean." Was this enough to convince Peter? No! The Lord had to repeat the scene two more times (which might be a great comfort to some of us)!

While Peter continued to question, three representatives sent by Cornelius arrived. Accompanying them to Caesarea, Peter was introduced to a large crowd of Gentiles—relatives and close friends of Cornelius. Cornelius offered a testimony, then Peter began to preach Christ. While Peter was still speaking (no time for discussion about unclean foods or holy days—and certainly no time for circumcision) the Holy Spirit fell on the entire group! Though totally shocked, that work of God's Spirit finally convinced Peter and those who accompanied him. "Can anyone keep these people from being baptized with water?" asked Peter. "They have received the Holy Spirit just as we have." So a great baptismal service followed—and the Gentile church was born!

Here is the irony of this whole scenario. Had Peter remained stubbornly unwilling to change any of his previously held opinions, none of this would have happened. It obviously forces me to wonder how much of what God longs to do among us, who so sincerely claim to want the Spirit's outpouring in a lasting and genuine way, has simply never happened because of our carefully defended unwillingness to change anything in order to pave the way for such blessing. What is, after all, really important to God—more important than all else? It has to be that lost people be brought to genuine saving faith in Jesus and receive His Spirit, for at that point eternal heaven and eternal hell are at stake!

I suspect it can be said of many of us that too often, we have been much more interested in "doing church the way we like it" than that unsaved people really find Christ. Is it change for change's sake we want? Not at all! But if we have "done church" for six months, a year or more, and no one has been converted, then the way we are doing church, no matter how much we like it, is not working! *Something* absolutely *must* change! Our matter of greatest concern then must not be whether we do or don't like the way we are doing church! We *must* involve ourselves in determining what must be changed in order to effectively reach unsaved people!

Peter faced that issue. And *he changed*—not the unadulterated message of Jesus! But he changed his attitude toward what he was willing to simply let God do without adding his own unnecessary requirements—requirements about which he held such strong opinions! One of the most pressing questions confronting the evangelical church today is, "Are we willing to do the same?"

SHALL WE BE CONTEMPORARY OR TRADITIONAL?

Read: Colossians 2:6-8

Who really wants change? I believe it was Mark Twain who said, "No one likes change except a wet baby!" None of us truthfully appreciates the necessity to drastically change *anything* which we have come to personally enjoy, think is right, or simply like!

At the same time most of us are asking God, quite sincerely, to work in our hearts genuine spiritual renewal. My obvious question has to be, "How can God do a biblical work of revival in *any* of us without some type of change taking place in our hearts, as well as in our daily living?" To plead with God for personal renewal with no actual expectation of changing anything is to effectively torpedo the very plea offered to God! Spiritual renewal always results in great positive *changes*!

A good friend of mine asked me, "John, since some type of change in the church is obviously necessary, just *how much* are you willing to see changed? How far are you willing to go?" I share with you my answer to him.

The *message* of the Gospel of Jesus does not change! We dare not alter it at all! But let's be very sure that we are, in fact, presenting the full, honest content of that biblical message in an uncompromising and understandable way. The *means*—the system or technique—we may utilize to present that message, on the other hand, may vary and change greatly. The types of music employed to demonstrate Gospel truth may be extremely diverse. The teaching methods may be altered dramatically and our preaching style modified. Brand new ways of presenting and clarifying the message may be introduced, but the message *content* of full salvation by faith in Jesus Christ alone must abide!

Beyond that, it is my conviction that *any attempted ministry*, inside or outside the church, which is not truly accomplishing the actual purpose for which it was brought into being must also be changed in one of four ways: it must be restaffed, refocused, replaced or dropped! In fact, when that which is designed to win the lost, build up the child of God or equip him/her to minister does not win or build or equip, some change is absolutely necessary! When such is the case, for the sake of the success of the Gospel and the genuine advancement of the Kingdom of Christ, let's get on with the changing!

But here is our problem. Lest those among us who might claim to be the most open to such needed change tend to become too enamored with our own inflated sense of adaptability, I state again, "None of us really *likes* change!" Even those who make the most noise about "the need for change," once having attained the desired goal, soon take their own places among those who are the most immutable at that point. It amazes me that the "contemporary drama presentations" and "worship choruses" (and styles) introduced a good number of years ago, and so well received by the church as a whole, are still being referred to as "contemporary" by many of those who introduced them. We fail to realize that, to so many who became believers at that time and who now may even be leaders in the church, their music and drama approach now forms their *traditional* style—the only one with which they have identified!

We know, too, that those who are insisting today we must "keep contemporary," in another ten years will be among the most conventional, enjoying *their* ten-year acquired change. Such will surely become flagrantly clear when, in that setting, a fresh breed of younger heads again emerges on the scene calling for their own new set of changes! And the cycle will begin all over again!

Here is the fact: *everything* contemporary soon becomes traditional. So let none of us become "overly righteous" or noticeably smug in either direction on this matter. Let us rather, choose to evaluate honestly and carefully whether what we are doing is really *accomplishing* what it was designed to accomplish. If it *is*, let us thank God sincerely and stay zeroed in on getting the job done! If it is *not*, or if an inordinate amount of our ministry is designed only to bless those who are already Christians with only a token effort being given to successfully reach unsaved people, let's pull together the necessary courage to effectively change what needs changing! Then let us joyfully get on with the greatest work in all the world!

ARE YOU EMBRACING "THE AGE WAVE" CHANGE?

Read: Psalm 71:5-9; 16-18

The Psalmist expresses one of the greatest concerns a person faces in the total grand challenge of living. David had passed through the shock of birth, the excitement of the ever new unfolding surprises of childhood, the learning developments and dangers of the youth years, the responsibilities of young adulthood and the satisfactions middle age affords. Now, as he pens the lines of the 71st Psalm, he is old and gray. Here is his prayer: "Do not cast me away when I am old, do not forsake me when my strength is gone...even when I am old and gray, do not forsake me, O God, till I declare your power to the next generation."

The desire to have an influence on the generation to come during one's latter years is a normal drive of that last cycle of life. This past generation has not always made it conducive for those who are "old and gray" to fulfill that natural longing. George Barna and Win Arn gave us some compelling facts about that age group a few years ago. The 76 million Baby Boomers born between 1946 and 1964 represent the largest generation in this country's history— "and," claimed Barna, "one of the most radical in their determination to define life according to their own desires." Moreover their children, though less numerous because of the birth rate decline among their Boomer parents, are having their own dramatic impact on the nation's marketers, as well as religious conscience—and will continue to do so for another ten or fifteen years or more.

However, almost unnoticed by a society geared to these younger interests, another slow but distinct change has been taking place among us which is certain to dilute and diminish to some degree the previously unchallenged influence of the "Boomers" and "Busters." People are living longer! Some experts speak of us as having entered the "age wave." The average life expectancy has increased to nearly 79 years of age. In the early 1960s five to thirteen year-olds numbered twice as many in the U.S. as those 65 and older. With the low birth rate between 1965 and 1980 and longer life spans, this has changed tremendously! Now there are more "Golden Agers" in our country than teenagers! What a compelling field for evangelism! In 1996 the Baby Boomers themselves entered their 50s!

What could be the potential of all of this? Well, consider the following: Bismark, who died at age 83, did his greatest work after he was 70. Verdi at 74 produced his masterpiece, "Othello," at age 80 "Falstaff," and at 85 the famous "Ave Maria," "Stabat Mater" and "Te Deum." Michelangelo painted the ceiling of the Sistine Chapel in Rome on his back on a scaffold when almost 90! My wife and I were privileged to see that great work while we were in Rome! Plus do not forget that Moses was 80 when God called him and, although he cited a number of excuses, "old age" was not one of them!

Here are some more eye openers concerning our own present day "65-and-older set" which the church must consider when planning future ministry:

1. The fastest growing age segment in America today, proportionally, consists of those who are 85 and older!

2. Between 1980 and 1990, the number of people over 100 more than tripled! Between 1990 and today, reaching age 100 is far less "newsworthy" than it was in either 1980 or 1990! Asked for his formula for long life, Dr. Arthur Judson Brown, Presbyterian minister celebrating his 103rd birthday, quipped, "Don't die!"

3. The number of people in the U.S. over 65 is now larger than the entire population of Canada!

4. Two-thirds of all the people who have ever lived to age 65 are alive today!

5. Every dollar being spent in the U.S. for consumer goods claims 41 cents from older adults!

6. Once a person reaches age 70 not having accepted Christ, the chances are about 1 in 120 that he/she will be saved!

The reason for the comment of number six may be surprising to us, however. After more than twenty-five years in the field of church growth, Win Arn concluded that the assumption that the older a person grows the more "hardened" he/she becomes is completely untrue! The lack of conversions among this group is not due nearly so much to a "fixed mindset to refuse" Christ's appeal as it is to *our own acceptance* of such a notion. It is our resignation to this idea that successfully stifles any of our intentional efforts to reach that age segment! Triple the efforts and we will see the results tripled. After all, Colonel Sanders of Kentucky Fried Chicken fame, was converted to Christ at age 79!

I fully agree with Arn's conclusion that in looking to the future, the church absolutely must adopt new priorities and strategies in programming for evangelistic and discipleship ministries which will make an ever increasing place for those who have introduced us to the recently recognized "age wave." May God help us to respond accordingly!

RELATING TO EACH OTHER

"It is impossible to learn anything important about anyone until we get him or her to disagree with us; it is only in contradiction that character is disclosed. That is why autocratic employers usually remain so ignorant about the true nature of their subordinates."

Sydney J. Harris
North American Syndicate
Quoted in READERS DIGEST

How Thankful Are You for Fellow Christians?
Can Others Afford to Imitate Us?
Can Disagreements Among Christians be Profitable?
Is There Room Among Us for "Lively Debate"?
How Much Respect is Due Your Pastor?
Who Is Listening Anyway?
Will Evangelicals Really Become Racially Reconciled?

HOW THANKFUL ARE
YOU FOR FELLOW CHRISTIANS?

Read: Romans 1:7-8; Philippians 1:1-4; 1 Corinthians 1:3-4

One of the characteristics we expect will mark the life of a Spirit-filled Christian is an attitude of thankfulness. Such a person has so much for which to be grateful. One very important area where that positive spirit invariably becomes extremely evident, and will probably be the most appreciated, is in the expression of thankfulness for his/her brothers and sisters in Christ.

Such a gracious attitude toward others, on the other hand, can hardly be thought of as an *automatic* outcome of being filled with the Spirit. In fact, many of us find that the automatic tendency is to focus on the negative aspects of our own lives as well as the lives of others. Thus we find it rather difficult to be truly thankful people. We are much more adept at complaining and griping—sadly!

It is to our chagrin that most of us, without much trouble at all, could sit down and scratch out a list of ten reasons why we have a right to complain about our circumstances involving others, but would be hard pressed to write down three valid reasons to be thankful. Why? Because we do, in fact, tend to focus on the negative things we see in others instead of the positive.

A mother said to her young son, "Joey, I'm so thankful for you when you are a good boy!" Joey wide-eyed and genuinely excited threw his arms around his mother and responded, "Mommy, I'm thankful for you all the time!" There it is! There is a difference, isn't there!

Paul was very open and free to express his thankfulness for his fellow Christians. He wrote to the saints at Rome, "First, I thank my God through Jesus Christ for you all" (Romans 1:8). To the Christians at Philppi he said, "I thank my God every time I remember you..." (Philippians 1:3). The believers at Corinth read his greeting: "I always thank God for you..." (1 Corinthians 1:4). Paul knew he had many reasons to express such gratefulness for these fellow believers!

At Rome the brothers and sisters were demonstrating a type of faith which was recognized and being spoken of throughout their whole world. The Philippian saints had expressed a special bond of love toward Paul. At Corinth the gifts of the Spirit were being manifested in a marked way. All this brought great thanksgiving to Paul's heart.

That is not to say, however, that these Christians were perfect people. At Rome, it is evident from Paul's letter that much correction was needed. Philippi had its Euodia and Syntyche who couldn't seem to appreciate each other. Apparently the whole church was well aware of their little feud. And we needn't look long to read of the problems among the Christians at Corinth! Jealously was evident. Divisions were clearly practiced—all on religious grounds, of course! They demonstrated a flabby attitude toward sin in the church and were bringing lawsuits against each other. Certainly Paul's thankfulness was not grounded in the fact that these Christians were all top-notch and very likable people!

Paul recognized the shortcomings of these children of God (and wrote to chide and correct them). But he also had a wonderfully big heart that enabled him, while not ignoring their need to be corrected, to focus on the positive aspects of their faith. In spite of the evidence of some very troubling problems in the lives of these people, he was able to be genuinely thankful for them—and to express it!

I believe it boils down to our "thought habits." We form habits of ungratefulness without much effort at all, don't we!? But it takes sincere prayer and conscious cooperation with the Holy Spirit to develop true thankfulness. That is why Paul has to admonish and exhort us not to be "anxious about anything, but in everything, by prayer and petition, with thanksgiving, present your request to God" (Philippinas 4:5-6).

Let it be our prayer that among us who are brothers and sisters in Christ, we will increasingly develop the good habit of being "thankful for each other." We belong to the same Heavenly Father. We love the same Lord, Jesus Christ. The one Holy Spirit lives in all of us. Let us say often to each other, "I thank my God every time I remember you!" Watch true unity be restored!

CAN OTHERS AFFORD TO IMITATE US?

Read: Acts 26:24-29; Philippians 3:12-17

"Hold your bat like this!" ordered the ten year-old would-be home run king to his buddy.

"I don't want to hold it that way," Jimmy retorted.

"But this is the way the major leaguers hold it!" the first shot back with as much cocksureness as he could muster.

"I don't care," was Jimmy's defensive response. "I don't want to be a copycat!"

There is a streak of Jimmy's spirit in all of us, isn't there? Most of us want to be more in life than a set of ditto marks!

Paul's remarks in Philippians 3:17 have been wrongly interpreted to call precisely for such mimicry. He exhorts the Christians at Philippi, and those of all ages, to literally "Be fellow imitators of me, brothers, and take note of those who live according to the pattern we gave you."

Does Paul's statement seem to smack of a streak of egotism? Not so! He only displays the same spirit he expressed in Acts 26:29 when Agrippa asked him, "Do you think that in such a short time you can persuade me to be a Christian?" Paul responded, "Short time or long—I pray God that not only you but all who are listening to me today may become what I am, except for these chains." He is saying, "I have become a true Christian, King Agrippa, and I pray that you will become what I am! I pray that all who are with you who are listening to me will do the same. I pray they will become Christ's followers as I am, but without the chains."

Paul had stated in the previous verses in the Philippian section that he had not obtained all that was obtainable spiritually, but he then says, "...forgetting what is behind and straining toward what is ahead, I press on toward the goal...." It is at this point that he urges his fellow Christians to imitate his example. Paraphrased, he is saying, "Fellow believers, you too, forget the past, strain toward what is ahead and keep pressing on toward the goal!"

Good example does, in fact, breed tremendous power! Tertullian, one of our great church fathers, stated that he and most of the converts who came out of paganism during his day, were won to Christ, not by books or sermons, but by observing how Christians lived and died.

A young man was invited at the last minute to preach at a church in Nashville and used the text, "Thou shalt not steal." The next morning he stepped on a bus and handed the driver a dollar bill and received his change. Upon counting the change, he realized the driver had given him a dime too much. Making his way back to the front of the bus, he said to the driver, "You gave me too much change."

"Yes, a dime too much," the driver replied. "I gave it to you on purpose. You see, I heard your sermon yesterday and I watched you in my mirror as you counted your change. Had you kept the dime I would have never again had any confidence in preaching."

"Unfair test," you might say!

Is it!? I don't think so. Here was a genuine test of honest, unguarded influence!

Certain people have stamped a lasting, positive influence for good on my life. I have taken note of their buoyant faith in Christ, their positive attitudes toward the will of God as they have understood it, and their goals to glorify Jesus and to attain to the resurrection from the dead. They have carved out a lasting impression on my life that has inspired a genuine desire on my part to imitate their example! I must insist, when I recall these godly, consistent models of grace, that it has not been so much what they taught me with their lips that has influenced me the most (though my appreciation for such teaching is not lacking). It has been what they taught me with their lives that has left the abiding impression.

Our lives will be influencing *someone* also! The question we must answer before God is this: "Can others *afford* to be fellow imitators of us? Can they *afford* to take note of those who live according to the pattern *we* have given them?" The apostle was confident enough concerning the pattern he and his fellow laborers had modeled that he felt he could well afford to prod them to imitate him. Let us be sure, by the help of the indwelling Holy Spirit, that our influence on others will be such that if some searching Christian among them should choose to imitate us, he or she would be safe and Christ would be truly honored eternally! So be it!

CAN DISAGREEMENTS
AMONG CHRISTIANS BE PROFITABLE?

Read: 2 Timothy 2:14-19; Romans 14:1-8

So long as we Christians, who would like to think of ourselves as students of the Bible, are clothed with humanity it seems quite unlikely that we will ever find it possible to come to complete honest agreement concerning certain practical and doctrinal interpretations of the Scripture. Does this tend to frustrate you?

Years ago, as a relatively new convert, I remember wondering rather naively, "If we all truly accept the Bible why can't we believe alike? Why are there so many differences of opinion? Who is right? Who is wrong?" It just seemed to me that if we all were truly sincere and honest we should somehow be able to come to the relatively same conclusions regarding these obviously important matters. Of course I also felt quite strongly that if we did come to agreement we would finally quite naturally, arrive at *my* conclusions. Now, after rubbing shoulders with hundreds of God's good people for a few years, I have discovered that there are very *few* people in the whole world who honestly agree with each other in every detail on *anything*, let alone on theological issues!

So it should not be surprising, after all, that two honest people may study carefully the same holy book and yet strongly disagree with each other in some of their interpretations of what they read in that book—a book which they both love and implicitly believe from cover to cover! Some of these dissimilarities surface in the various shades of teaching regarding such subjects as the perseverance and preservation of the saints, predestination and the sovereignty of God, free will, sanctification, the second advent of

Christ, the phases of the judgement, the methods of water baptism and the gifts of the Spirit. All evangelicals accept these doctrines, but varying emphases exist in applying them.

At various times in the histories of nearly every denomination and independent group in existence, a call has come to re-examine one or more of the various theological tenets espoused. I am convinced that such strict self-examination, if guarded and not carelessly habitual, can be good. It has the potential of forcing the exercise of intellectual honesty in our understanding of the Scripture. This has to be commendable! It may or may not prompt a modification or clarifying of some particular statement. If it forces us to think more clearly (and possibly more honestly) it has done what it has been designed to do.

In spite of such periodic examinations, however, obvious diversities of opinion have, and always will, exist between God's people. This is not sinful—it is healthy! It should help us all to think more carefully, pray more earnestly and study more diligently, endeavoring to understand scriptural truth as it truly is, unmodified by our prejudices (which we all have) and our theological biases. This is the honesty to which I refer—and which I pray we can all develop!

Some of the most invigorating and profitable discussions I have had, have been with those whom I genuinely respected, but with whom I thoroughly disagreed. And, believe it or not, fellowship was not lacking! Great spiritual enlightenment for my own soul was realized! It seems to me that the Christian community would certainly be an uninspiring place if every member in it understood *everything* just as I do! Where would be the challenge to one's intellectual capacity to think in such a setting? Where would be the incentive to any spiritual vigor?

Who among us really desires to be part of a mutual admiration society, where we all live under a false impression of "peace with each other" only because we have accepted the numbing notion that God makes all saints on an assembly line basis? Is it really to be expected that we are all to act alike? Look alike? Sing alike? Pray alike? Believe alike? React alike? I think I would have my fill of being a part of such a community in less than two days time!

The sin that plagues evangelical Christianity is not that we disagree with each other in some of our explanations of Scripture. Rather it is that we have allowed a subtle pride in our own opinions to diminish and, too often damage our genuine respect for those with whom we find ourselves in such disagreement.

The fact that we may differ with each other in some of our teachings gives none of us a license to degrade the other or consign each other to a lower plain of spirituality or commitment. Must we accuse each other of dishonesty? Let us rather, in humility, strive to heed the sublime injunction of a very wise man of a former day, to simply "agree to disagree agreeably."

The God-given right to disagree is a wonderful blessing! Let us put this privilege to use wisely and freely where conscience demands, without apology or fear of intimidation. But let us also use this privilege respectfully!

On the other hand, let us never fear to have another disagree with us. To differ and to be differed with can drive each of us to our knees in earnest search of unadulterated truth—and that is an immeasurable blessing!

IS THERE ROOM AMONG US FOR "LIVELY DEBATE"?

Read: Acts 15:1-21

Very early in my Christian pilgrimage I developed a rather blurry hunch, due to a naive perception, of what I thought the results of a Spirit-controlled life should be. I assumed that internal controversies were stifled to a bare minimum in the Spirit-filled church the apostles organized following that momentous Pentecost day. I rather imagined if even the semblance of a potential problem dared to raise its head among such God-fearing people, they probably simply, but sincerely, prayed and God's love melted their differences into placid serenity and agreement.

Then I read in the scriptures what really happened! In Acts 15 Luke records that, early in the church's history, controversy did erupt in the church. Fostered by one large group among the new believers, the issue which surfaced was the teaching that one could not be saved apart from being circumcised according to the custom taught by Moses. Soon Paul and Barnabas found themselves locked in the middle of heated debate with that segment of the church. The church determined that Paul and Barnabas, with other believers, should go to Jerusalem to the apostles and elders where a conference was called. The "whole assembly" (NIV) gathered for the discussions.

It is quite obvious, even in the midst of the exciting reports of evangelism given by Paul and Barnabas, that emotions ran exceedingly deep and opinions were very strong involving the issue to be discussed (Acts 15:5). Words like "great dissension and debate" (NASB), or "sharp dispute" (NIV), describe the scene which preceded the conference. The expression "much disputing" (KJV), describes the conference itself. Peter, Barnabas, Paul and James seem to have led the voices on the prevailing side of the "lively debate" (Berkeley), but it is extremely clear that they were not the only ones who spoke to this very important doctrinal issue.

What was the outcome of such a spirited public exchange of opinions? Well God, as He has been prone to do on quite a regular basis throughout church history, overruled the strongly opinionated views of people! He did, in fact, bring a sense of harmony in their conclusion which "seemed good to the apostles and the elders, with the whole church" (Acts 15:22, NASB). We do not know for certain just how they arrived at that decision. Whether by vote or by general consensus or some other means, agreement was reached as to what should be written in a letter to be sent to the churches—and that agreement was accepted as the will of God.

Evangelical denominations and associations across the U.S. and around the world still experience such "lively debate" periodically in their regularly scheduled national conferences. Sometimes the issues are every bit as important as the issue which these apostles tackled. No doubt, at other times, our emotions are greatly stirred over debatable questions which are of very little interest to God at all! But we still encourage such discussion and even "sharp dispute." It forces us to keep sharp in our thinking. Hopefully, it drives us back to the Bible, the Word of God, for our conclusions!

My denomination, the Missionary Church, has engaged periodically in rather emotional disputing—even some dissension at times—over such issues as the second coming of Christ, the imminency of the rapture, sanctification, the security of the believer, spiritual warfare (the Christian and demons), the role of women in ministry, biblical inerrancy, oath-bound secret societies, and the Lord's Day. But in the very throes of such fervent discussions, we too, have heard exciting reports as did the apostles, of some of the results of strong local evangelism and intensive church planting! Many new churches and thousands of new believers have come into being. The expansion of overseas missions has excited us.

Have all such conference votes resulted in all the members becoming convinced of the correctness of the decision? No, that is
too much to hope for—just as the Jerusalem decision did not reap
such results. Entrenched groups persisted in teaching the necessity of circumcision even following the conference. But the official position of the church was settled!

Ah yes, let us continue to debate and let that debate even fan
our emotions at times! But let us also be praying sincerely that
when all debate subsides and decisions are to be made, God will
also continue to bring as much harmony as possible to our conclusions, as He did in Jerusalem, which will "seem good with the
whole church." As those early Christians did, let us also accept
such decisions of our praying body of delegates as the will of God
for us at this point in our historical pilgrimage.

But in the very throes of such fervent discussions, let us also
hope and pray for more exciting reports, as did the apostles, of
strong local evangelism and intensive church planting as well as
successful missionary outreach. Let us pray for thousands of new
believers to come into being! Grant it, Lord!

HOW MUCH RESPECT IS DUE YOUR PASTOR?

Read: 1 Thessalonians 5:12-13; 1 Timothy 5:17

The call of the Lord placed upon the heart of a person by the Holy Spirit to pastoral ministry is a high and holy calling. We who claim to be followers of Christ need to be reminded to guard a very positive attitude toward the pastors He has selected to minister among us. We must aggressively promote an intentional willingness among us to treat our pastors with honor, love and respect. Paul writes, "But we request of you, brothers, that you appreciate (respect) those who diligently labor among you and have charge over you in the Lord and give you instruction, and that you esteem them very highly in love because of their work..." (1 Thessalonians 5:12-13). "The elders (pastors) who direct the affairs of the church well are worthy of double honor, especially those whose work is preaching and teaching" (1 Timothy 5:17).

One of the seven promises which "Promise Keepers" has enjoined upon the men who participate in the commitment involved is this: *"A Promise Keeper is committed to supporting the mission of the church by honoring and praying for his pastor, and by actively giving his time and resources."*

In issuing this call I do not assume that the pastor is always the most spiritual person in a local congregation, nor do I affirm that his are always the best decisions rendered or his ideas the most visionary. I know the pastor can, at times, be defensive and less than spiritually motivated in some of his efforts. He may even merit a well-timed rebuke given in a sensitive way by the properly appointed person(s) and at times owe his own apologies to people. But, recognizing all of this, I remind us that the pastor is, never-

156

theless, under God and, in most cases, by the selection of the congregation, the leader of that body of believers!

Sometimes it seems to me that I sense among a percentage of
us in evangelical churches a rather smug attitude. Here it is: If a
local pastor does not keep pace with the beat of certain recognized
lay persons in a given congregation—whether in what he preaches,
or the way he does his work, or for even daring to assume that he is
in fact the spiritual leader of the flock—he will, in a very brief
time, be called up for vote and drummed out! That attitude, no
matter how we may attempt to justify it, does not please God and
is wrong! It has, when persisted in, never failed to hurt the local
church in the long haul. If it ever becomes the accepted attitude in
general in any denomination or group, God will as surely as He
has placed His hand of blessing upon that body in a unique way,
just so surely lift that hand of blessing which is now enjoyed!

Scripture holds us responsible and accountable, personally and
corporately, to render to our pastors at least seven things: We are
responsible to *respect them* (1 Thessalonians 5:12), to *love them*
(1 Thessalonians 5:13), *honor them* (Philippians 2:9), *pray for them*
(Romans 15:30), *encourage them* (1 Thessalonians 5:17), *submit
to their leadership* (1 Corinthians 16:15-16) and *adequately support them* (Luke 10:7)!

I personally, have wonderful and positive memories of a band
of people who made up the local congregation in North Manches-
ter, Indiana, where I was sent at the time I entered the ministry in
1959. I was young enough to be a grandson to some of them. But
they volitionally purposed among themselves that they would love
and respect my wife and me and fully accept us as their pastor and
wife. They could have faulted me often, but instead they prayed
for me so faithfully and counselled me when I was about to make
a foolish decision. They had patience with some of my periodically unguarded statements and believed in my sincerity. They
made me feel good about being their pastor and let me know that,

with all of my shortcomings, they were proud of me as their pastor and proud of my wife. I bless the memory of those good people! They could have broken me. They helped grow me instead and truly helped me become a preacher!

What would it do for your pastor—and for your church—if a team of seven men would unite together to meet at regular times to pray consistently for him, such as on Sunday morning before the message, again on Sunday evening and at least once during the week? What would happen if members of the church you attend would divide up the days on the calendar in such a way that two persons would pray for your pastor's specific needs every day of the year? What might transpire if every strong-headed layman in any association of believers would intentionally choose to recognize his pastor as God's appointed leader for that body of saints at this time in the congregation's history? Why not try it and find out?

My prayer is that my denomination will become known in evangelical circles as a denomination of people who love their pastors! We are blessed with some of the finest in the country! Ask, "Why not bless them and see what God does for both them and us?"

WHO IS LISTENING ANYWAY?

Read: Proverbs 1:5; Luke 8:18

"Who is supposed to be talking here?" blurted out one exasperated member of the local church elder board during the most animated segment of heated debate. "I am!" The answer erupted simultaneously from the frustrated pastor, the confused chairman of the committee which had introduced the controversial issue and the officious elder whose ministry would be affected. "So who then is listening anyway?" asked the originator of the question. "Who indeed?"

The fact that the senior pastor is the God-appointed leader of the local congregation obviously does not authorize him to "force" his will ex cathedra style on any board or local membership—that is dictatorial! No, on the other hand, does any lay leader's position excuse intimidation as a maneuver to muster followership. True leaders, clergy or lay persons, are those whom others *choose* to follow because they have earned their respect through consistent example. They fully understand that one of the greatest strengths of a biblical leader is found in sincerely *listening* to fellow believers.

Embarrassing derailment certainly awaits the would-be Christian leader who is convinced that he is so "tuned in to God" that he has no reason to actually listen sincerely to anyone except those who agree with him. James, the brother of our Lord, offers some very sensible words in the epistle which bears his name. "My dear brothers, take note of this: Everyone should be quick to listen, slow to speak..." (James 1:19). Whether or not James had ever heard the well known quotation from Zeno of Citrium, I do not know. In 300 B.C. Zeno is supposed to have said, "The reason we have two ears and only one mouth is that we may listen the more and talk the less." Someone of lesser repute has said, "Talk and you say what you already know, but listen and you learn something new." Whether pastor or lay person, leader or follower, we all need to hear this admonition.

One afternoon as Charles R. Brown busied himself in his office at home his five year-old son joined him with an armful of toys. Mike played—mostly he talked. "Daddy," he said.

"Ah-huh," Charles replied.

"Daddy!" Mike persisted

"I'm listening, son, while I'm working here."

"No, Daddy," retorted a determined son. "Listen to me with your face!" Ah! There is the secret of listening!

Ever notice how often you and I totally "block out" the thoughts and ideas of would-be fellow communicators? I do not mean we don't quite understand what is being articulated. I mean, while we feign attention, our mind is engaged—consciously or unconsciously—in solving other problems, or formulating our answers to yet unasked questions, or trying to unmask what we think is *really* being said.

In the busyness of involvement with important things, I sincerely wonder how many opportunities I have missed throughout my life to engage in real life-changing dialogue—with my children, with my wife, with true friends! How many times have I glided right over the top of such dialogue because I "heard" what I was preconditioned to hear, or because I simply heard what I wanted to hear? I am forced, during periodic examinations of my own heart, to deeply regret how often I have settled for something less than the best communication with the most important people in my life. I wonder how often I have missed a very personal message from God Himself due to my rapt attention being fixed on issues of much lesser importance. The irony is I will probably never consciously "miss" what it was God wanted to say to me. No wonder Jesus has implored all of us to "...consider carefully how (we) listen" (Luke 8:18).

What more may be said if this same mindset of failing to listen persists during times of renewal in our local church or during board meeting discussions and debate, such as depicted above, regarding potential for future dynamic ministry and outreach? Our personal privilege of sharing in the blessing of such renewal and potential outreach will probably be chucked also. And again, the real disaster will be that we will never realize our loss! The church will go on—and we will marvel at the alive ministry success—but it is unlikely we will be able at all to really share personally in that excitement.

Of course, listening does not always presume agreement with what is truly heard. To assume, for instance, a pastor is not listening simply because he chooses on an occasion not to do as advised is unfair. Listening does, on the other hand, involve a sincere intentional effort on the part of that pastor to truly understand what the one endeavoring to communicate is actually saying—and why—whether he finds himself in agreement or not! So truly listening is the issue! Who is listening? That is, after all, the question!

Why listen, pastor? Why listen, lay leader? Let the wisest of men answer: "Let the wise listen and add to their learning, and let the discerning get guidance" (Proverbs 1:5). Why not listen a little? We just might learn something?

WILL EVANGELICALS REALLY
BECOME RACIALLY RECONCILED?

Read: Acts 17:24-28

The Chicago Joint Conference on Racial Reconciliation spon-
sored by the National Association of Evangelicals and the National
Black Evangelical Association, January 6-7, 1995, for me proved
to be an exceptionally enlightening time—and equally frustrating!
It made me uncomfortable. More than 170 evangelical leaders
grappled with the issues identified with the sin of racism, and dia-
logued in an atmosphere of great candor regarding the real costs of
genuine racial reconciliation.

I had long been convinced that I am not a racially prejudiced
person—certainly not bigoted! I had periodically spoken out, quite
forcefully I might add, against attitudes and practices which I perceived to be racist. So why then did the conference make me so
uptight? By the time we were midway into the proceedings of the
first day of that conference I had become very uneasy with the
disillusionment expressed by my brothers and sisters of color concerning times of *previous* dialogue with dedicated Caucasian
evangelicals. Why this semi-skepticism? These meetings had produced no follow-through type of action! At first I was quite surprised—then became convicted—by their disappointment with
extremely busy white evangelicals like myself who were so correctly engaged in battle with so many of the immoral practices of
our day, but who were at the same time so obviously detached
from those morally devastating issues involving racism.

I was, in short order, awakened to many of the hurts festering
in the very souls of some of my black, as well as Hispanic, fellow-

believers, but from which my own uninformed response mechanism had kept me so carefully and safely guarded. I began to feel that I had quite possibly been, in some ways, a type of biblical "tourist." I had been adept at carefully observing and explaining Scripture texts which deal with the sin of racism as I "passed by." But I had never really planned to "get involved" within the boundaries of the implications of those texts to really "live there." I wondered whether black evangelicals might have had the correct term, after all, when they called my solemn pronouncements and all the duly passed resolution statements I had helped vote through "platitudes?"

Mind you, I still do not accept the accusation that this obvious disconnectedness between what we were maintaining to be our inner convictions and what we habitually performed in our outward actions had been primarily intentional! But *that*, after all, was what made our problem so knotty then—and sadly, still does to this day! Our professed beliefs may be sincere. But our observable behavior, though not deliberate still does not express in any appreciable way to believers among minorities those solemnly held sentiments!

So what steps can we who really want to facilitate racial reconciliation take to correct this issue? Let me suggest four:

1. Let's purpose to take as many intentional steps as necessary to allow the Holy Spirit to replace any trappings of racial arrogance we may be secretly nursing within us with a genuine biblical respect for the dignity and equality of every individual God has created. Let us recognize that God "made from one man (blood) every nation of men."

2. Let's exercise intentional correction of the type of personal faith that may have become so comfortable—so crusted—as to cause us to really not *want* to be disturbed with "one more moral struggle,"especially one that would cry out for some priority time!

3. Let's sincerely endeavor to develop a relationship with at least one person of another color and communicate in a meaningful way with that person at least once a month. Let's discuss our developing kinship with another person of our own color, encouraging that person to establish his/her color link.

4. Let's take the necessary risks involved to combat any latent fear of potential intimidation from good friends who, for whatever reasons of their own, may totally misunderstand our attitude and actions regarding racism.

Let us from our perspective, at least *begin* to foster a genuine racial reconciliation climate among evangelicals!

DOING THE WORK
OF EVANGELISM

"Every member of the church—in fact, *every believer*—ought to know how to share his or her faith. If Christians are to penetrate the community with their witness they must know how to share Christ with others."

Samuel D. Faircloth
Taken from CHURCH PLANTING
FOR REPRODUCTION
Baker Book House Company
Copyright © 1991
Publication rights returned to
Samuel D. Faircloth
Used by permission

Are We Doing the Work of Evangelism?
Who Will Do the Work of Evangelism?
Can We Afford to Let God be God?
How Attractive Shall We Make the Gospel?
Who is Concerned About Growth?
Do I Believe in Church Planting?

ARE WE DOING THE WORK OF EVANGELISM?

Read: 1 Thessalonians 1:6-10

"Evangelism" has been an increasingly popular subject for a number of years. Both mainline and conservative denominations have discussed the issues and drafted resolutions relating to this type of work. During one year recently American Baptists, at their national convocation on evangelism, issued a press release calling the church to evangelize. The United Church of Christ, at its mission conference, did the same. Later that same year the Episcopal Church held an evangelism and missions conference—the first of its kind organized outside its General Convention, and by the following September, Southern Baptists had called an evangelism meeting with evangelical para-church groups and representatives from the United Methodist, Presbyterian, Mennonite, Assemblies of God and Nazarene churches. That was quite a year for public statements and definitive ecclesiastical dogma regarding evangelism!

The question to which we must respond, however, is this: "In the midst of discussing evangelism, issuing press releases and attending conferences (all of which I believe are important), are we, in fact, actually *doing the work* of evangelism?"

Depending upon who the expert is or what the perspective of the would-be evangelizer might be, evangelism can fall under many descriptive titles. To some it may refer to an approach as soft as nonverbal witness. To others it embraces hard-sell conversion. And yet another group focuses on social action and feeding the hungry, while their counterparts envision church growth and gaining new members. But do all—or any—of these descriptions truly depict what is involved in biblical evangelism?

The New Testament word from which we derive our English verb "evangelize" means "to proclaim the glad tidings"—any good news—but especially that of Jesus Christ! The good news about Jesus was to be given in such a way that unbelievers would be moved to repent and by faith receive through Christ the forgiveness of their sins.

The Christians in Thessalonica exemplified this "work of evangelism" in an outstanding way. Paul writes, "The Lord's message rang out from you not only in Macedonia and Achaia—your faith in God has become known everywhere. Therefore we do not need to say anything about it, for they themselves report...how you turned to God from idols to serve the living and true God..." (1 Thessalonians 1:8-9). Just how they made the good news known, Paul does not state. However, we do know that Thessalonica was a bustling trade center. Traders entered the city on a regular basis to hawk their wares. Can we doubt that many of these new Christians dealt with these traders and effectively shared their new found faith with them? Were they impressed? Apparently they returned to their home areas spreading the news of the new converts wherever they went! When Paul traveled into these areas he found he didn't have to say anything about it, for the news of Jesus had preceded him—spread by others who had heard it from the Thessalonian Christians! What a model of evangelism—of "proclaiming the glad tidings!"

While the call of the Lord to evangelize is given to some in particular (Ephesians 4:11), His general call is to every one of us! All Christians are called to be filled with the Holy Spirit and to be Christ's witnesses (Acts 1:8). The individual believer who shares the good news of Jesus with an unbeliever, with the intention of bringing that person to saving faith, is doing the work of an evangelist. The husband and wife who invite their neighbor couple over for an evening, with the purpose of building bridges and eventually winning them to Christ, are doing the work of evangelism.

Conversely, any work, the final intent of which is not to bring lost people to Christ, is not truly evangelism! It may be useful. It may even be extremely important in the total ministry of the church (or of an individual). But let us recognize that, though also greatly needed, it is not evangelism. For the same reason, some of the descriptions which some groups have given to depict evangelism, listed above, in the true sense of the term are not evangelistic though they also may be very needful.

The intent of my concern is not to determine whether or not other such types of ministry are important. My forgone conclusion is that they are! However, I'll repeat the question with which we must contend: "In all the important types of work we are doing, are we proclaiming and sharing the good tidings of Christ in such a way that the unconverted are being led to saving faith in our Lord?" Is our witness by both clergy and laity seeing unbelieving people repent and believe to salvation—along with other expected results? By definition, the work of evangelism is intended to draw the lost to personal salvation in Jesus Christ. In all of our activity, let us be sure that we are also doing an effective work of evangelism!

WHO WILL DO THE WORK OF EVANGELISM?

Read: Ephesians 4:11; 2 Timothy 4:5

The pivotal point of my life came on Sunday morning, Mother's Day, 1951. At the close of the morning service during special evangelistic meetings, and following the message of a visiting evangelist, I went forward and knelt at the altar at the front of the Osolo Missionary Church in Elkhart, Indiana, and committed my heart to Jesus Christ. Those were the days when "evangelistic" meetings were more closely aligned to being just that. Many more unbelievers came to the services than do now. "Evangelistic" meetings more recently have come to be "renewal" times where Christians are brought to confession, invigoration of faith and encouragement. These times are so important! But few, if any, nonbelievers are involved in any way—or even present.

On the other hand, the genuine biblical renewal so desperately needed periodically among us, ought surely to result in some type of effective evangelistic outreach ministry! After all, who is to do the work of evangelism? Some would affirm that the better question is, "Who is *not* to do the work of evangelism?" The original verbal equivalent in the New Testament for "evangelize" is one of a number of terms usually rendered with the simple English word "preach" and signifies, as pointed out in the previous reading, "the announcing or telling forth or preaching of the Gospel."

It appears that Paul used the noun form of this term in two ways. First, he referred to a particular group of those proclaimers of the Good News of Jesus who were designated specifically as "evangelists" (Ephesians 4:11). In Acts 21:8 those who accompanied Paul on his missionary journey to Caesarea entered the house of one who was called "Philip the Evangelist." Clearly the term came to be employed as the identifying reference to a special class of those who announced the life-changing message of our Lord. They were uniquely gifted by the Holy Spirit for such a role. Their calling was to proclaim the glad tidings to those who did not know such truths rather than to give instruction and pastoral care to those who had believed and been baptized. Their task was to reveal to unbelievers the claims and benefits of Christ. They did so with the intent of being used by the Holy Spirit to convince them to turn from their unbelief to positive repentant faith in the Savior for salvation.

The second way Paul used this term was more open. It is clear that in a general sense, *anyone* who proclaimed mercy and Gospel grace to non-Christians was considered to be doing "the work of an evangelist." Timothy was most certainly not, in the strictest sense of the word "an evangelist." Yet Paul wrote to him urging him to "do the work of an evangelist" (2 Timothy 4:5). Though not occupying the official position of an evangelist, he was also to be about the work of endeavoring to convince and win unbelievers to Christ. He too, was carrying out the work of evangelism as an *unofficial* evangelist.

Both of these aspects of the work of evangelism are very much intact today. The Holy Spirit still calls and equips certain of Christ's followers to conduct a full-time ministry geared intentionally to the primary task of reaching and winning unconverted people to Christ. Some are traditional traveling itinerant messengers of God. Others go to inner cities as committed personal workers. A few are Christian dramatists and musicians. The ministry of one evangelist in the denomination of which I am a part is that of a public academic lecturer, debater and author who, on many leading college campuses, debates some of the leading atheists and agnostics in the U.S., Canada and Europe with the view of convincing non-believers. These servants of Christ deserve our strong prayer, financial and moral support.

But the work of evangelism is not theirs alone. All believers, to one degree or another and in one way or another, need to be making the Good News of Christ known to unbelievers with the intent of influencing them to faith. An increasing number of local churches in the U.S. are gearing the entire scope of their ministries to a three-fold purpose—to *win, build and equip* people to serve their Lord. The *building* and *equipping* aspects of the work are being more and more focused upon adequately preparing God's people to know how to *reach* and *win* unbelievers to Christ, as well as to serve in other areas of their giftedness.

I appeal to us to fully recognize our obvious need to utilize the ministries offered by God's specially called and gifted "evangelists." I also appeal to all of us who have come to faith in Christ, that we too, shall be intentionally involved in some way, according to our various gifts, in doing "the work of an evangelist." Together, let us evangelize!

CAN WE AFFORD TO LET GOD BE GOD?

Read: 1 Corinthians 9:21-23

Some lessons are very difficult for Christians to learn. One seems to be this: God is not a set of ditto marks! He seldom moves among His people in precisely the same way He did during the previous generation.

In every dynamic outpouring of the Spirit in revival and renewal, which has then resulted in effective evangelism, there have invariably been some resulting incidents and a few new methods of ministry introduced which have caused the rank and file of the existing church to become very uptight! The apostolic church, consisting primarily of Jewish converts, didn't quite know how to respond to Paul, who was continually moving away from their respected but unnecessary traditions, in order to reach as many as possible for Christ, including Gentiles. The Roman Church did not know at all what to do with Martin Luther, much less Menno Simons! Charles Wesley greatly irritated the church leaders of his day (with John's blessing) when he put "Christian" words to barroom tunes and used them in worship so the common people could become familiar with the words more quickly. These later came to be some of the very hymns which we sing with deep reverence today.

Then there was D. L. Moody who was too uneducated to be ordained and too willing to give to a Catholic fund-raising project to please Protestants of his era. The Catholics generously reciprocated, however, and some were converted! Billy Sunday's "tiger in the cage" pacing and chair-waving acrobatics embarrassed far too many decent church folk of his day, and Billy Graham has endured the.wrath of more than a few fundamentalists for his co-operative methods. But the uncompromising message of salvation delivered by all these men was clear, and the unsaved were won to Christ! However, without exception, each "did things" much differently than those who preceded him. God chose to mightily use the entire lot to convince unbelievers to believe!

Here is the issue: biblical evangelism, by whatever format, has one focal point. It is intentionally structured toward unsaved people aimed to convince them to turn to Jesus Christ for the salvation of their souls! We claim that the work of evangelism must be top priority on our list of ministries! On the other hand, we have all discovered that it is far easier to write evangelism into our list of "top priority ministries" than it is to truly "make evangelism a real priority" in our actual performance of ministries. Herein lies the tension! It is easier to discuss—to argue—the pros and cons of the various methods of evangelism than to actually get about the business of doing it!

We can become so convinced that the way *we* "do things" is the only way upon which God can really smile. He who dares to try anything in a different way simply cannot be seen by us as having God's full blessing. Our sanctified prejudices may become the most dramatic thing about us! We can totally forget at times that God has never obligated Himself to "check in" with any of us before He plans to break upon us in a brand new exciting way. Do you know what happens then? He simply sends His Spirit to do His work. And if we are too biased and closed to the methods He chooses to use, He is obligated to walk right past us and get on with what He is doing at that point in history—without us! He will not be forced to ask the permission of any of us to do His own work! After all, it is *His* work!

Format, though important, simply cannot be the final issue in the work of evangelism. By whatever method(s), the bottom line question must be, "Are unsaved people coming to the Lord Jesus?"

If the program we are using is resulting in a good number of such victories, let us be grateful to God and double our efforts! If on the other hand, the specific method we like is not convincing unsaved people in our area to come to Jesus, then for the sake of these lost people let us be willing to lay aside our own preferences and try some other more effective format which will actually reach and win these people in our city or community to Christ.

The fact is, in evangelical churches and groups all across our country and around the world, the Holy Spirit is choosing to do lasting work through methods some of us are not accustomed to—methods some of us may not prefer. How shall we respond? Our foremost attitude absolutely must be to willingly and gladly "let God be God!" Paul's statement is still extremely pertinent: "I have become all things to all men so that by all possible means I might save some. I do this for the sake of the gospel, that I might share in its blessings" (1 Corinthians 9: 21-23). It will take an abandoning of those carefully cradled prejudices—sometimes even our simple preferences—to simply allow God to do His work in His way. We have said it often to each other—do we really believe it? "The methods will change! The message forever remains the same!" Can we afford to truly be willing to "become all things" to those for whom we are responsible, that "by all possible means" we might "save some?" The better and more pertinent question, obviously is, "Can we afford *not* to?" Let's actually let God be God and make evangelism a real priority!

HOW ATTRACTIVE SHALL WE MAKE THE GOSPEL?

Read: John 3:16-19; Romans 8:6-9

It is exceptionally easy to become deluded concerning just what constitutes our God-given task as heralds of the message of Divine grace.

That we live in a consumer-driven society is well understood. The assessment of our appeal to that society, according to certain segments of the church, will more and more be based solely on our ability as dispensers of the good news of Jesus, to respond to a well entrenched "consumer mentality." People's "needs and desires," self-centered or not, will continue to clamor for our undivided attention, notwithstanding the fact that what the unregenerate (or even regenerate) may "want" is not always what he/she "needs." The cry will be for us to endeavor to satisfy the unbeliever's personal need for "a sense of well-being" whether the utter commitment of a saving heart faith to which the Bible calls all of us is present or not. If we respond affirmatively to that cry, the sacrifice of self-surrender will itself surely be called upon to surrender to the seeker's "right to self-fulfillment."

"What we need to do," we hear, "is to alter our presentation of the Gospel" so as to somehow make the good news we share "attractive" to unbelievers. Am I then to understand that part of our task is to *make* people to whom the call to surrender is *unattractive*, "want" Christ? Just how attractive are we supposed to make the Gospel? Does the Gospel's "attractiveness" finally depend upon "how we present its truths?" As loaded as these questions are, I offer them!

That there is a right and a wrong way to present Jesus to misguided and unbelieving people is a given! There is a sensible and wise way to present Christ, as well as a radical and insensitive style. One wins! The other repels! Both are in great use today!

But when all is said and done—even when said and done in a careful and sensible way—calling people to turn from their sins to trust Christ alone for salvation is not an automatically attractive message to the person who still takes pleasure in that sin! Jesus said, "Men love darkness instead of light because their deeds were evil" (John 3:19).

Many years ago in the classroom of a godly professor named Wayland, a student rose to ask the following question: "Dr. Wayland, if Christians were more amiable, kind, lovely in their dispositions and in their relationship with the world, and if they presented Christianity in its true aspects, don't you think everybody would be so attracted and charmed as to embrace it at once?"

Dr. Wayland became very deliberate and earnest as he formulated his reply: "There was once on earth One who combined in perfect symmetry all the graces of Christian character; One who was wise, kind, unselfish, lovely, without fault, and absolutely perfect. And what was the result of this exhibition of character in the world? They cried, 'Crucify Him! Crucify Him!'"

We might add to Dr. Wayland's statement that there were eleven apostles who, though not without fault as their Leader, yet lived as unselfishly as any have lived since. They made this Gospel as attractive as anyone could—or should—make it. Yet how did the world react to their lives? Tradition declares that all except one died violent deaths at the hands of wicked men, and John missed such a death only by a miraculous escape from a boiling caldron of oil.

There lived a missionary who reached all of his then known world, making this Gospel as attractive as a consecrated life was and is able to make it. Nevertheless, the apostle Paul lost his head on the chopping block! There was an era when the Christian Church was more pure and attractive than it probably has ever been since. Yet those saints were thrown to hungry lions and burned at the stake.

There exists a biblical principle which we are so prone to forget. The apostle himself penned it for us to remember: "The sinful mind is hostile to God, it does not submit to God's law, nor can it do so" (Romans 8:7). When an individual is ruled by a carnal heart, no approach or method is "attractive" enough to *make* that person want what he/she, by nature, does not want! The basic need is not that people will be *attracted*, but rather that they will be *awakened*! That calls for the Divine intervention of the Holy Spirit! Our *real* task is not to some way attract unbelievers, but to earnestly pray that the Holy Spirit will awaken them to their lost condition.

We simply cannot afford to forget that the great transaction of regenerating those who are dead in trespasses and sins is not our work. It is the work of the Holy Spirit! He does, in fact, work through the influence of His human servants, but it is *His* work! It is ours to pray earnestly and to witness faithfully; but it is His to awaken and regenerate! When the inner heart is truly awakened by the Holy Spirit, then—and *only then*—does the Bible message become truly attractive. Let us recall, for years the news of Jesus was not very attractive to us. Then one day we became drawn to its offer, not because the news was different, but because the Spirit of God made us different. He awakened us to our undone state, our helpless condition, our landslide to a lost eternity. He helped us understand that our inner longings for fulfillment could only be truly met in Him! Then Christ and grace became attractive! So shall it ever be!

WHO IS CONCERNED ABOUT GROWTH?

Read: Acts 2:41-47

My concept of "growth" involving the body of Christ is two-fold. *Spiritual growth* is evidenced by the believers who make up a congregation becoming more and more like Jesus. *Numerical growth* follows when those believers reach out to non-Christians with a caring witness of the Gospel resulting in unbelievers coming to faith. So I maintain it is extremely important that local churches do, in fact, become *growing* churches!

In Luke's account in Acts 2:4 and 41 we read that the disciples were filled with the Holy Spirit (that is *spiritual* growth). The results? Three thousand people were converted upon hearing their witness (that is *numerical* growth)! We read that the newly Spirit-filled followers of Christ "devoted themselves to the apostle's teaching, and to the fellowship, to the breaking of bread and to prayer...with glad and sincere hearts, praising God..." (Acts 2:42-46). What clear evidence of *spiritual* growth! And what was the result? *Numerical* growth! "The Lord added daily to the church such as were being saved" (Acts 2:47). On one occasion during this time Peter and John while on their way to the temple to pray, became God's agents for the healing of a man crippled from birth. This miracle attracted a crowd and Peter preached the resurrection of Jesus. Their obedience to Christ landed them in jail (Acts 3:1-4:3). But this obedience in the face of trouble also evidenced continual *spiritual* growth. Following the miracle of healing, the number of men grew to about five thousand (Acts 4:4) —again, numerical growth! Yet further, we read that when they were threatened and persecuted they purposed to "obey God rather than man" and "rejoiced because they had been counted worthy to suffer disgrace for His name," and "they never stopped teaching and proclaiming the good news that Jesus is Christ" (Acts 5:29, 41-42). Here again is obedience under fire. Is this not *spiritual* growth? Ah yes! And look at what followed—*numerical* growth: "The number of disciples was increasing" and "multiplied" (Acts 6:1,7).

Clearly Luke measured in a positive way, the growing strength of the work done by the apostle believers by the increasing number of persons who were converted, baptized and added to the church. The "number of people," while not the bottom line measurement of the spiritual progress attained, was nevertheless, important enough to the Holy Spirit that He prompted the writer to record it for posterity for all to read and profit thereby. Apparently someone "took a count" or gave a careful estimate—or possibly the Holy Spirit simply revealed the numbers to Luke as he wrote (in which case I would *really* be impressed). In any case, the growth in the number of the people did, in fact, serve as one measuring rod of God's blessing!

All things being equal, genuine spiritual growth will invariably lead to numerical growth. It seems to me that every pastor and local congregation leader should be convinced that God's clear purpose is for their churches to grow intentionally! Our reason for desiring such numerical growth must, however, be pure! If our motive is simply to feel the excitement of having more people or to be known as a growing church or to feel the pride of success, we have totally mutilated the only valid reason to work for growth.

Our sole reason for desiring and working for continual numerical growth is this—every person without Christ is lost! I am very much aware that evangelical people claim to believe this. However, I fear much of the time we do not behave as though we do. I am convinced that God, by His Spirit, wants to help us recognize the desperate need for believers to reach out to as many unsaved people as possible with the good news of salvation. As local congregations conduct such ministries of evangelism, surely growth, both spiritually and numerically, will result.

No wonder not one word is recorded of Peter becoming nervous over what to do with "all these people" when three thousand persons repented on Pentecost Day. We read nothing of his becoming fidgety over "the problems that would result" when the number increased to five thousand some weeks later. When the Lord "added daily to the church those being saved," and when the number of believers "was multiplied" we do not read even a hint of "growing too large," or "too fast for their own good."

Did the explosive growth result in some problems? Of course! But the problems took second seat! Why? Because every person was recognized as one for whom Christ died and who needed to be saved. Eventually they worked together to solve the problems (Acts 4:32-37; 6:1-6). But they did not allow any of the problems to deter them from continuing to spread the good news of Jesus with the intentional purpose of seeing more and more unbelievers come to Jesus Christ (Acts 5:12-14; 6:7).

Who is concerned about growing? God is! Here is our mandate! Here is our task! Let us rise in the power of His Spirit to meet our challenge—and be about the business of growing, all to the glory of God!

DO I BELIEVE IN CHURCH PLANTING?

Read: Titus 1:1-5; 1 Corinthians 3:6-7

Do I believe in church planting? Of course I do! I believe the Church of the Lord Jesus Christ must continue to be very serious about planting new churches, first, because I am deeply convinced God is calling us to do it! (Matthew 28:18-20). Quite obviously, that is reason enough for me!

But I also have a very personal—sometimes very emotional— reason for believing in church planting. My very first recollections of "going to church and Sunday school" are of playing in a sandbox in a preschool/primary class in a basement church building on the northeast side of Elkhart, Indiana. Our family had been invited to this Sunday school somewhere around 1941. My mother responded to the invitation and took my brother, my sister and me along. This became the beginning of what my family thought of as "regular Sunday school attendance"—every other Sunday or so.

This basement building congregation was "born" some seventeen years previous to my sandbox experiences, a result of the concern of a good grandmother in the neighborhood and one other worker from the town of Elkhart. They didn't call it "church planting" back then. In fact, by today's definitions it probably would not have been called a church plant anyway. It was a mishmash between a fledgling "community Sunday school" and a sometimes independent community church which invited preachers from the Baptists, Methodists, Seventh Day Adventists, United Brethren, and Mennonite Brethren in Christ to minister to the people.

In 1944 this struggling cluster of believers chose to unite with the Mennonite Brethren in Christ denomination (later known as United Missionary) which was destined to be one of the two denominations (the other—the Missionary Church Association) which merged in 1969 to become the Missionary Church. Under the blessing of faithful gospel preaching, the congregation experienced unusual growth! My mother was one among the increasing number who came to Christ!

My remembrances of those early Sunday school experiences are very positive. To this day I feel extremely fortunate to have been included in the fruits of the ministry of the Osolo Missionary Church congregation. Osolo was ahead of its time. I became one of the "church bus kids" before church buses were popular. Contests were the order of the day! Those were the days when 61 percent of the Sunday school population involved children. Pastors worked overtime trying to get adults to come to Sunday school, hoping an increasing number would remain for the worship service. The attendance of the Sunday school was always much higher than that of the worship service.

During our "growing up years" my mother made certain that her three children were in Sunday school quite regularly—though our worship attendance fluctuated more. Into my teen years, the Holy Spirit began to press the claims of Christ on my young heart. At the close of the morning worship service on Mother's Day preceding my sixteenth birthday, during a special revival effort (I had decided to remain for the service for my mother's sake), I stepped out with about fifteen or twenty others to kneel at the public altar, and commit my heart to Jesus Christ! This was the point of "turn-around" in my life! My sister was also converted at the same altar that morning.

Through the years much has changed in the way the Osolo Church has done ministry, as it has in the majority of evangelical churches. Busing, so dominant and successful then, is not effective at all now. Very little enthusiasm could now be generated for "winning a contest bike or Bible." And since the early 1970s, the worship service has passed the Sunday school, averaging 25-40 percent more in attendance than its former leader, though many more adults are also now attending Sunday school (or its replacement) than during the 1940s and early 50s.

The Missionary Church has experienced some marked changes in emphasis in the various phases of its ministry, as have many other evangelical denominations. The worship services are aggressive, and for the most part, growing. Discipleship has become extremely crucial. Music is more upbeat and probably more contemporary blended with the former Gospel songs and hymns. We are on the cutting edge of church planting. The work of missions has zeroed in more on "unreached people." Winning unbelievers to Christ, and building and equipping Christians for the service of Christ have become the driving issues. Ministering to the real and special needs of people, shepherding the body of believers and recognizing and utilizing our Spirit-given gifts for the sake of the entire body have all become very important.

Do I believe in church planting? Oh yes I do! But my belief in church planting is not motivated by a desire to simply "build and count more buildings." Building Christ's Church is not a matter of erecting more buildings. It involves reaching and winning more *people* to Christ! I am a part of the kingdom of Christ Jesus today because of the efforts of those few very committed people on the northeast side of Elkhart to plant a church as they understood how to do it back then! It was the sacrifice of those people, who made a floundering basement Sunday school in the late 1940s and early 1950s into a part of what is now the Missionary Church. It was their perseverance that led to my salvation! I bless their memory, as well as the continuing ministry of that congregation to this day!

ASSESSING WORLD MISSIONS

"The essential issue is this: To what extent are we as a mission organization committed to responsible participation on equal terms with the existing Christians within a target country? Can we join hands to such an extent that we are willing to let our own plans and strategies die in the process of building a movement which can be something stronger and greater?"

James F. Engle
Taken from A CLOUDED FUTURE
Copyright © 1996 by
Christian Stewardship Association
3195 S. Superior, Suite 303
Milwaukee, WI 53207
All rights reserved. Used by permission.

Is Missionary Work Really Worth It?
Can a Blind Man Really See?
Hearing, Will They Believe?
Is it Fair?
Do You See the Emerging New Face of Missions?
Are We Up to the Worldwide Task?
What Persecution?

IS MISSIONARY WORK REALLY WORTH IT?

Read: Isaiah 52:7

During the explosive 1970s when an inordinate percentage of 20 to 30 year-olds were hiking around the States "trying to find themselves," a young Nigerian preacher came to the U.S. to enter Bethel College in Mishawaka, Indiana. Jacob Bawa had been born into the Kamberrie tribe in the rural town of Salka. His mother died when he was eight days-old, and an aunt rescued him from being buried with her (a heathen custom of those days) and raised him in the pagan practices accepted by his society. When the government decreed that every compound send one of its boys to the public school for education, family members chose ten year-old Jacob, over his aunt's protests, to be enrolled. The school, located 30 miles from Salka, was operated by Moslems and to enter the system "conversion to Islam" was required. His "baptism with water from Mecca," however, according to his own testimony, changed Jacob only "from a dry sinner to a soaked sinner!"

It was through the witness of a Christian Kamberrie friend back in Salka that Bawa, at 16 years of age, attended a service in the Missionary Church. There, for the first time in his life, he heard missionary Isabelle Hollenback give the good news of Jesus! "I watched the Christians singing joyfully," says Jacob, "and the Word took hold of my heart. Jesus spoke to me telling me I needed him as my personal Savior." One week later the same friend took him to another missionary, Art Reifel, who led him through John 3:16 to repentance and faith in Christ for salvation. "As soon as we finished praying there was a great change in me!" states Bawa with a genuineness in his voice. "He changed my heart and I found a peace and a joy that I had never had before!"

He began to grow spiritually, and as the years passed, he relates, "The Missionary Church built me up solidly in the Lord." After graduation from the Missionary Church Theological College in Ilorin, he returned to his home town of Salka to become the pastor of the church and principal of the Hausa Bible School. Following a year at Emmanuel Bible College in Kitchener, Ontario, and a time of teaching at the Theological College, he returned to EBC to earn his bachelor's degree. It was in connection with this time of study that he came to the U.S. to take special courses at Bethel College, then moved on to further study at Trinity Evangelical Divinity School in Deerfield, Illinois. He entered Michigan State University for the completion of his M.S. and Ph.D. and finally returned to Nigeria to become the first national president of his denomination, the United Missionary Church of Africa. When Billy Graham preached in Nigeria, Jacob served as his interpreter.

At this point a radical change in ministry took place in Bawa's life! Nigerian government leaders recognized his unique giftedness and approached him for government service. With the full blessing of his denomination and God's approval, he accepted the challenge. Following stints as his state's Superintendent of Public Schools and Secretary of Education, he served as registrar for the Federal University of Service and Technology and chairman of the Niger State College of Education Board.

In 1987 the head of the Nigerian government appointed Jacob as Nigeria's ambassador to Spain where he interacted with King Carlos, and to the Vatican where he was privileged to bear witness of his faith to Pope John Paul II. At the Vatican, the Pope presented Bawa with a Merit Award, distinguishing him as the best ambassador during the term he served. He also met with the Queen of England, and later served as ambassador to the Republic of Chad. In these government positions Bawa exercised overwhelming influence for God and good affecting these countries. He also brought about tremendous religious and educational changes in his own country. "I felt I was not only my country's ambassador," he states, "but also an ambassador for Christ."

Following his service to his country's government in 1995, Jacob returned once again to the United States with his wife, Rose, as a visiting professor at Bethel College in Mishawaka, Indiana, to teach religion, philosophy and education, and to minister in churches across the states as requested. "The Gospel of Christ" has always been his message, and serves as his motivating drive as he makes plans to return to his homeland to fulfill his dream of opening a Christian school. Rose shares this call with her husband, and will be an integral part of this venture.

Do you think evangelical missionary work is actually worth the money and effort? When Jacob hears this question his eyes widen and his demeanor betrays personal conviction. "Your work in missions has not been in vain!" he asserts. "My own ministry has been possible because you sent missionaries to my country! If you had not done so, I would not have come to know Jesus Christ as my Savior!" To Jacob Bawa, that is enough to make it worth it all!

CAN A BLIND MAN REALLY SEE?

Read: Matthew 13:11-15; John 9:25

One of the happies, and most victorious Christians I knew while serving as a missionary in Nigeria, West Africa, was blind Wurjanjan. He lived in the large Kamberrie village of Salka. His testimony rang with authenticity as he would raise his voice in praise, both in the Salka church and in the town itself. "I thank God! I thank God!" he was heard to say many times a day.

It had not always been so for Wurjanjan. Thirty years before I met him he had left his compound in French-ruled Africa and set out to find money. Coming to Nigeria, he traveled from place to place in his hungry search to attain wealth. He had farmed. He had worked in gold and tin. He had raised cattle, baked and built huts and compounds.

In the providence of God he found himself in the village of Salka where he worked for the chief. Through the years, however, sin had taken its toll on his life. Like many of the heathen, he became a slave to beer. Every market day he would drink his beer, and then lie in the market in a drunken stupor throughout the night until someone would carry him to his hut in the morning. Even his heathen friends, who themselves drank a lot of beer, were embarrassed and laughed him to scorn.

Wurjanjan knew of the work of the United Missionary Society (now World Partners of the Missionary Church in the U.S. and the Evangelical Missionary Church of Canada) and the United Missionary Church in Salka, but had no contact with the mission personnel. Then one day he heard that the mission was planning to build a second house on the compound and he applied for work. He was hired and worked hard. Immediately he began to hear about Jesus Christ. But this news was so new to him that he was not much influenced beyond periodically attending a few services. How could someone who lived so long ago, and whom he had never ever seen, possibly change him into a new person?

But something drew him back, and as he came to the services from time to time, the Holy Spirit began His reliable work. The faithful witnessing continued. And though it sounded so strange, that message, as it has done in the hearts of millions of people from every type of culture in every country in the world and in every age, began to grip the heart of Wurjanjan. He couldn't completely understand his own feelings, but he knew he was becoming convinced that the Jesus way was the right way.

One Sunday, to the surprise—even shock—of everyone present, Wurjanjan stood publicly and declared, "I want to repent." Could this actually be for real? Was Wurjanjan truly sincere? Did he, in fact, even understand what it meant to "repent?" God, Who knows the inner heart of every person, saw the desire of this African heathen man and knew he wanted to receive Christ and be changed. The three missionaries then stationed at Salka gathered and prayed earnestly for him, and the God of all mercy reached down and touched Wurjanjan's heathen heart and worked a marvelous miracle!

Immediately Wurjanjan began to witness to his new found joy. Now his heathen friends laughed again and began a different kind of mockery. But time began to prove—even to them—that this man really was different! He was, without a doubt, truly a new man!

Assurance of salvation in his heart was very real. He could not read, but he listened intently to the reading of God's Word and the preaching in the church. Carefully he obeyed the Spirit. He began to pray regularly, and the Holy Spirit strengthened him in his new walk with his Savior.

Before his conversion Wurjanjan had become infected with tapeworm which had affected his eyesight. Shortly after his spiritual eyes were opened, his physical eyes closed in darkness. When I knew him he had not seen the sun for fifteen years, but he had beheld the Son of righteousness rise with healing in his wings. With face aglow and heart ringing, he would say, "You see, I am a blind man, but in my heart I see! Through faith I see!"

Wurjanjan never found money—but he found the One Who owns the cattle on a thousand hills! For the remainder of his life he laid up treasures in heaven! His life consistently demonstrated that an African villager could exude true happiness though he was not wealthy in an earthly sense and though he could not see physically. A grandson led him to church, and around the village of Salka on the end of a stick. But Christ Jesus led him in the way everlasting by His own powerful hand.

A few short years after my wife and I left Nigeria to return to the United States this happy blind man closed his sightless physical eyes for the last time—and opened his spiritual eyes in Paradise—and saw Jesus! I think I can still hear him saying, "I thank God! I thank God!" Rejoice on, Wurjanjan! You have a long forever to give vent to your eternal happiness!

HEARING, WILL THEY BELIEVE?

Read: Romans 10:12-15

The year was 1965. The setting was Nigeria, West Africa, in the northwest village of Raba. God had placed this community on the hearts of the missionaries and the African pastor in the nearby town of Salka for many months. In Raba a small group of seventeen Christians had maintained a witness. In the early 1950s, Rev. Art Reifel had visited the village and a church was begun. But progress had been slow, and for a number of years there had been no pastor to shepherd the flock. Courageously these believers had stood firm in spite of the negative influence of the pagan and Moslem forces in the entire area. They had gathered every Lord's Day to worship in their little church the best they knew and understood.

Though paganism was extremely strong, Jacob Bawa, Salka's pastor at that time, knew that there were many young men in Raba who had begun to realize the folly of their heathen practices. They were "hanging in the balance" between the truth of Christianity and the lure of Islam. Then one of these young men repented and found Christ! Pastor Bawa and the missionaries became convinced that the time was right to move in with a united effort to win the other young men before Satan gained the victory by drawing them into Islam.

As plans were laid opposition arose. The chief and the village fathers, members of one of the two fetish religions in the area, refused to consent for their meetings to be held in the village proper. "We do not have big gatherings to spread our pagan religion," they argued. "Why should we consent for you to spread yours?"

The Christians decided to move the meetings to the space in front of the little church itself. What at first appeared to be a hindrance became a blessing in disguise, for those who were genuinely interested came to the edge of the village to hear the messages. Those who would have invaded the meetings in the village proper only to disturb did not show up outside the town.

So during the first week of February that year the missionaries, Pastor Bawa, the Salka Hausa Bible School students and some of the Christians from the Salka church climbed into the cab and back of the Dodge pickup mission truck each evening to drive to Raba. There they united with the Christians from Raba for the open air meetings. Many unbelievers came! From the village came the Kamberries, and from the fields came the Fulanis, to listen to the records being played over the loudspeaker and to hear the Christians sing and testify and pray. They listened intently to the messages given by Pastor Bawa.

Many of the young men for whom special prayer had been offered came also—and they, too, listened carefully. As the messages were given the Holy Spirit began to rivet the simple truths of the Bible to the hearts of the listeners. These young men, one by one and in twos, began to think seriously, then remain after the meetings to repent and believe. The believers rejoiced as a total of seven of these young men of the village found new life in Jesus Christ!

As the weeks passed following the meetings, more of the other young men were also awakened to their need of salvation. Likewise, young husbands and wives began to confess that they wanted to follow the Jesus Way. It did not happen all at once. They came, two by two and three by three, to repent. Seldom did a week pass, however, that Pastor Bawa did not receive word that at least one had trusted Christ at the weekly meeting of the Raba Christians. The converts witnessed to other friends and relatives and they too, came to faith. A little more than a year later forty-five adult Christians were worshipping at Raba and a Salka Bible School student had become their student pastor! What great encouragement this brought to the 150-160 Christians in Salka, as well as to the remaining 80-90 believers represented in the six other churches of the Auna/Salka/Kontagora area!

Now, here is the bottom line question: Did that marked move of the Spirit bring any changes to that part of Nigeria on a long term basis? Fair question! The answer is just as fair! As you now read this account, more than three decades have come and gone. The entire Auna/Salka/Kontagora area has been powerfully affected by the witness to the truth of the Gospel of Christ on the part of the ever growing body of believers in this part of northern Nigeria! Kontagora is now a district of churches itself! The Christians in Raba have rebuilt their church many times as the building became too small for the growing number of believers! The first district superintendent for the Kontagora District was a convert from Raba. A number of pastors have been converted here! More than 265 persons worship each Sunday in the new church which is now there! Three churches exist in Salka itself, two of which average 1,200 persons apiece on each Lord's day, and the third, 800! A fourth church will be having weekly services when this is read. Besides this, two other churches identified with missions other than the one with which I am associated exist in Salka. In the total area more than 8,000 Christians worship in 70 churches identified with the Missionary Church (from 50 to more than 200 persons per congregation)! The two pagan fetish religions are all but nil. Islam remains, but its grip on the people is not strong. There are so many churches that plans for this area to be divided into two separate districts are in place, each with its own district superintendent.

Ah yes! The preachers were sent! The people heard the Gospel! Upon hearing, they truly believed—and were saved!

IS IT FAIR?

Read: Matthew 9:35-37

Before going to Nigeria, West Africa as a missionary I had often wondered in my young aspiring heart what it might "feel like" to be the one who presented Christ to some certain people who would be hearing about him *for the very first time*. "I wonder what it would be like," I would ask myself, "to know they who had never heard before would hear from my lips!"

In the middle 1960s, we who labored in northern Nigeria were vividly aware that there were yet areas essentially untouched by the Good News of Jesus! This fact especially gripped me while I was spending six days working with one of the pastors in the village of Tungan Bunu. Tungan Bunu was located on the edge of one of these areas—a vast 1,300 square mile triangular region where the Achifawa and a few of the Dukawa people groups lived. They were completely unevangelized, though in the 1940s missionary Russell Sloat had cycled through the area to preach and survey. Since then no one had returned. This group was not the same immediate tribe as the Kamberries located in the Salka area where Retha and I lived and taught in the Salka Hausa Bible School. Neither were they identified with the Agwara tribe located west of Salka, though it seemed quite certain to linguists at that time that during previous generations they were all three one people.

About twenty-five of these Achifawas had brought cotton to sell at the Tungan Bunu market, but those who dealt in cotton had run out of money. So these young men found it necessary to remain in the village for three or four days waiting to be paid. When the local pastor heard this news, he immediately invited them to come to hear "the young American with white skin" tell good news from God. And, to our joy, they came! They didn't know how to act in the building called "a church." They simply lined up along the back wall, decked in their market finery of masculine jewelry, feathers and all!

I remember praying in my heart as I spoke, "Lord, surely these men haven't heard about you very often. Help me make this news of Jesus known in a way that is understandable to them." But it was evident that they understood very little. However, I was deeply impressed with their careful attention. They returned! And they listened so intently! Between services there was time to get better acquainted.

I asked them, "Have any of you ever heard about this man named Jesus before now?"

One responded, "I think possibly I have—at the house of medicine (mission hospital) in Tungan Magajiya. I think the one they talked about is the same one you are telling us about."

I assured him that He was the same person. All of the remaining men answered, "No, we have never heard about this man before!" I finally realized how one would feel giving the message of Jesus to people for their first time! They assured me they would keep coming to the meetings as long as they were in the village. And they did! "If we keep coming," said one, "maybe we can begin to understand your teaching." When they sold their cotton they returned to their scattered villages in the interior. I never saw them again.

I remember yet the question which plagued my mind during this incident: "Is it fair that those on the edges of this great triangle hear the message while those represented by these men—the people of the whole interior—never hear at all?"

I knew even then that the answer to this problem would not be found in simply sending more missionaries into that region. We missionaries knew that the greatest need was for national workers to be willing to make such areas *their* field of service! Nigerian converts who lived in the cities and larger towns would have to be willing to sacrifice the security of their own communities and tribal surroundings to enter such needy parts of their native country and live with "their own" who were so unlike them. But the national church had not at that time caught the vision yet for such outreach as they have in more recent years. It did not happen.

These men, and now their children and grandchildren, and the entire people they represent, still inhabit this same 1,300 square mile triangle, living in scattered hamlets. Twenty-one years after the incident I described above little had changed. In 1987 when Rev. Art Reifel, with two pastors and some Hausa Bible School students drove and walked all through this entire triangle to share the news of Jesus, it was still completely unreached. Sadly, they met only one man in all their travel who had ever heard of the Savior, Jesus Christ. Where the men were to whom I had preached twenty-one years previously, I do not know! For all these years this neglected people group was not influenced at all by the life giving Word of God. I was still asking, "Has this been fair?"

Then, in 1990, Nigerian evangelists began to work in some of the villages in the triangle. That year the first converts came to Christ! Missionary Lois Fuller visited throughout the area during the following couple of years. In 1992 a church was started by a national church planter, and by the next year twenty-nine Achifawa tribes people had become Christians. Today evangelist Joseph Dazi maintains about one hundred Achifawas are serving Jesus Christ! They have finally heard! They are believing! The number is increasing! God is breaking down the long held barriers! To Him be praise! Has it been fair? No! But it is changing for the better— and for that I am grateful.

DO YOU SEE THE EMERGING
NEW FACE OF MISSIONS?

Read: John 4:34-38

The past twenty years worldwide growth patterns in the evangelical church have painted a new face on this segment of Christian believers. A marked shift has taken place involving the very "global center" of Christianity.

Our history reveals quite factually that through the years, the church has seen a steady increase in the number of Christians throughout the world. During the past two decades, however, that sheer number growth has exploded in an astonishingly dramatic way! A tremendous move of the Spirit of God in select countries around the world has resulted in a phenomenal count of unchurched people being brought to Christ. According to Stan Yoder, former World Missions Center representative, the 78,000 new Christians in the world every day reported by Chris R. DeWett in GLOBAL CHURCH GROWTH back in 1988-89, could even be higher today!

However, what American evangelicals are failing to realize is that the greatest percentage of this evangelical growth has not occurred among us in North America and Europe (not even combined), but rather in Asia, Africa and South America. For the past number of years the world's largest church has been the Yoido Full Gospel Church in Seoul, Korea (around 1 million members). The next two largest are in South America: The Evangelical Cathedral of Jotabeche in Santiago, Chile (more than 480,000 members), and the Vision of the Future Church in Argentina (nearly 150,000 members). In the early 1990s Bishop Abel Muzorewa of the United Methodist Church in Zimbabwe, and a former prime minister, was stating that more than six million people were being converted to Christ in Africa annually! When missionaries were forced to leave China in 1949-50, they left one million Christians. Today, reliable China watchers conservatively estimate there are nearly 50 million. The Chinese State Statistical Bureau puts the number at 63 million!

In 1970, two out of three persons in the entire evangelical population on our planet were in the Western World (United States, Canada and Europe). By 1980, it was half Western and half non-Western. Today, more than 70 percent of all evangelical believers live outside of North America and Europe, and that percentage is increasing constantly!

The down side to all of this good news is that in spite of all the growth in the worldwide evangelical church, and using the broadest definition of the word "Christian," only one-third of the world's population can be considered Christian at all. Two-thirds of our present world is still unevangelized! The world birth rate is still outstripping the conversion rate. The Great Commission is still in force!

There is no question that the long-term shake-out of the shift taking place will emerge in a sharply defined way in the years ahead. As the challenge of world evangelization becomes greater, one of the most exciting aspects of modern day missions is the growing strength of the third world church. Increasingly, this segment of the universal Church of the Lord Jesus Christ is mobilizing to become a mighty "sending" agency. Those who were once the "recipients" of missionaries are now preparing to send missionaries to other needy areas of the world. Strong leadership among this new exploding segment of the evangelical world is already emerging. They reflect a missionary agenda which portrays the culture, conditions and challenges found in non-Western countries. Many missiologists are convinced that the day is coming when the third world church will be the leading sending agency for missionaries. Adjusting to and becoming part of this new agenda will be one of the greatest challenges of the Western evangelical church! Time will tell whether or not we have the spiritual fortitude to make this necessary adjustment.

The question is, obviously, "How will we respond?" If we in North America expect to continue to play a significant role in evangelizing the world, we must choose to accept these inevitable changes gracefully. While focusing intentionally on the unsaved and unreached, we must purpose to encourage and cooperate with this non-Western world evangelistic thrust. Such an effort with these new world evangelical churches and mission organizations, which may accept our help but not our control, will be a brand new uncharted course for us in the West. Let us pray for increasing wisdom and courage as we become a part of God's new agenda for worldwide evangelization!

ARE WE UP TO THE WORLDWIDE TASK?

Read: Acts 12:24-13:3

Any person "in touch" with the present "missionary climate" is much aware that the entire missions enterprise is changing in some very dramatic ways. There is increasing momentum today in the work of missionary evangelism being done in a number of countries. Evangelicals, as might be expected, are doing by far, the lion's share! It appears more and more, however, that this driving force of evangelism is not being shouldered with as much intensity by the Western church as it is by evangelicals in the two-thirds world. This is not to assert that our passion is gone. It is simply perceived by some to be fading. We do know that it is not at all unusual to read of mission agencies in the U.S., Canada and Europe which have plateaued, both in terms of personnel and finances.

Some missiologists, and a few denominational leaders in the U.S., are beginning to wonder whether it is not possible that our very long held "missionary philosophy" itself has, in fact, inadvertently *contributed* to this very decline in missions passion which we now are beginning to decry! A primary ACTIVE/PASSIVE philosophy has driven us in our missionary work from its inception. The primary recognized task that the Western evangelical church considered "essential" to fulfilling the Great Commission, was to "send out missionaries" and to "pay their expenses." Thus, mission organizations originally came into being with the purpose to *actively* "recruit and dispatch workers" who took the message of Christ to an unreached world. The personnel of the home churches, however, inherited the *passive* role of "senders and supporters." They depended on the mission groups to "do the work of missions."

The missionaries were forced, by the very circumstances of the unreached fields, to play the dominant role in all the ministries performed. They pastored churches, taught school, did medical work, built buildings, did clerical work, baptized new believers and much more! They did a tremendously good job! All around the world, in previously totally unevangelized countries, the Church of the Lord Jesus came into being! And it grew! Circumstances began to radically change. In some of these countries outstanding national leaders emerged to assume the leadership previously performed by Western missionaries. Today there are a number of missionary sending countries with maturing churches which are more and more assuming the initiative to reach their own people and those of other cultures.

HERE IS OUR PROBLEM: In spite of these focal changes in the evangelical world, we in the West still tend to insist on "doing missions" by the same ACTIVE/PASSIVE philosophy! But informed Christians in our local churches, who travel much more now than formerly, have seen the "overseas church" in action! To them, being passive "senders and supporters" simply cannot be fulfilling any more. If they are going to pay, they will also have to be able to be more involved! They will more and more have to be convinced that their funds will not be invested in North American families being sent to do what the national church can already more effectively do itself.

WHAT HAS TO HAPPEN AMONG US IN THE WEST TO SEE OUR PASSION RETURN? First, we must recognize that Western Christians, while still intent upon being sure that missionaries will go to truly *needy* places in the world, nevertheless, are going to be unhappy being only "senders and supporters." Instead of being "agency *dependent*," they will desire more "church ownership" in the *total process* of motivating, selecting, sending and placing of missionaries! Increasingly they will want *their* missionaries to be sent only through those agencies which will properly "match" them with the work nationals cannot do themselves.

Local churches will develop a vision to "adopt" some of the unevangelized people groups, zeroing the greater part of their missions personnel and ministry in on these groups. They will form teams to visit fields. There will certainly be less and less interest in an organization that is primarily interested in the church only as "a source for funds and personnel."

Secondly, we in the West must recognize that the role of Western missionaries is radically changing! They will not be going to countries where the national church is already established to do "the traditional type of pioneer missionary work." They must "come alongside" the national leaders, at their request, and be willing to work under their direction, to help train new national leadership. They must offer specialized and enabling services that will help the national churches truly reach their own countries and beyond! The "authority issue" must, increasingly, be truly transferred to the national leadership for work done under the auspices of the national church.

Thirdly, we must recognize that in spite of the tremendous move of the Spirit throughout the world, there are still 2,000 ethnolinguistic or ethnic people groups which have no viable congregation of evangelical believers among them! Though many of these are extremely difficult areas, we must intentionally focus our efforts much more on *these* people groups! Obviously, no one church or denomination can reach all of them. Much more *cooperative pioneer work* will be necessary by both Western and third-world agencies to reach these peoples!

What an exciting day to be involved in the great worldwide work of missions! Are we big enough for the task? Are we flexible enough for the necessary changes? Are we committed to Christ enough to see true "kingdom work" completed? We *must* be or we could be out of business! God help us!

WHAT PERSECUTION?

Read: Matthew 5:10-12; 1 Peter 4:16-19

Throughout our history the evangelical church in the United States has been uniquely privileged to work and evangelize in an atmosphere which has been relatively open. Though we have experienced many more restrictions in the last decade and a half than we had previously been accustomed to, and though we have become greatly concerned about what future restrictions or freedoms may develop (some of us have urgently complained periodically to our elected officials), we nevertheless have experienced much freedom. We tend to be totally oblivious to the fact that we still enjoy far more liberty to proclaim the Gospel of grace in this nation than the vast majority of our brothers and sisters in Christ do in so many areas around the world!

We U.S. evangelicals have been woefully ignorant of the suffering that thousands of people in other countries are facing right now merely because they have faith in Jesus Christ. The silence on our part before governments and media (and even before God) has not been the result of a lack of concern. We have simply been out of touch and unaware of the facts! This is to our chagrin!

The last 25 years have seen a massive growth of evangelicals outside the Western world. I remind us again from a previous reading that today more than 70% of all evangelical believers live outside the West in the two-thirds world under less than truly democratic regimes. These numbers continue to grow at a staggering rate according to OPERATION WORLD by Patrick Johnstone. On the other hand, this growth has also been accompanied by a sharp rise in Christian persecution in an inordinate number of areas around the globe, though largely unnoticed by us.

World Evangelical Fellowship (WEF), with whom the majority of evangelical denominations are associated through our National Association of Evangelicals, gives us some startling information. James and Marti Hefley, in their book BY THEIR BLOOD, maintain that there have been more people martyred for their faith in Jesus in this 20th century than in all the previous 19 centuries from the time of Christ combined. The statistical research of WEF Religious Liberty Commission shockingly reveals that more people have died in circumstances related to their faith during this time than in all the wars of this same 100 year period! Though it seems unbelievable, WORLD MISSION DIGEST claims there have been 100 million martyrs in this "civilized" 20th century!

The United Nations reported in 1996 that the militant Islamic government of central African Sudan had, years ago, declared systematic battle against Christians. Between 1982 and 1996 300,000 Sudanese Christians were killed. And it may be shocking to the majority of us to hear that reported incidents of persecution worldwide have actually increased since the fall of Soviet communism. It is well established that the house church movement in China suffers continual persecution—even torture!

Only recently I, as did a number of other leaders of evangelical denominations in the U.S., wrote a strong letter to the Crown Prince and Prime Minister of the State of Kuwait. On May 29, 1996, Robert Hussein, a Kuwaiti citizen who had converted from Islam to Jesus Christ, was convicted in a Kuwaiti religious court of "apostasy" and the judge ruled under Islamic law he could be killed. Such a verdict served as the equivalent of granting open encouragement for any radical branch of Islam to carry out the sentence. Robert was forced into hiding while the church around the world mobilized to respond to his plea for safety from militant Islamic groups. Evangelical leaders called for the Kuwaiti government to publicly state that they will honor their constitution which allows religious freedom for all. We could only hope and pray that such a united outcry from around the world would cause the instigators of such inhumane nonsense to back away from their intentional purpose to stamp out the Christian witness! However, in this case, it was to no avail. The pressure was too great and Robert, whatever his original motives were, recanted. Renouncing his testimony of faith in Christ, he returned to his country and Islam pleading for his safety. This case was lost to the cause of Christ. Many others are facing courageously the threats of their very lives, and maintaining firm faith in Jesus.

We U. S. evangelicals must become more aware of the plight of fellow Christians in other countries! At the very least we *must* pray more! In April 1996, the Religious Liberty Commission of WEF called for an International Day of Prayer for the persecuted church to be held annually on the last Sunday in September. The goal is to have multiplied thousands of evangelical churches in more than 100 countries all praying on the same day annually for believers who are suffering because of their faith in and testimony for Jesus Christ. While being willing to "suffer for His sake," surely sincere united prayer can effect a marked reduction in such incidents of radical persecution against the people of the Lord. At the same time we dare not allow our thinking here in comfortable America to become so alienated from the higher thoughts of God that we forget the words of Peter: "However, if you suffer as a Christian, do not be ashamed, but praise God that you bear that name. For it is time for judgement to begin with the family of God...So then, those who suffer according to God's will should commit themselves to their faithful Creator and continue to do good" (1 Peter 4:16-17, 19).

EXAMINING HIS BIRTH
AND RESURRECTION

"On the resurrection hangs the legitimacy of the Christian faith.
Whether the incarnation is more important than the resurrection
or the resurrection more important than the incarnation is a moot
issue. Without either of these significant events, there would be
no hope for sinful humanity."

Kent D. Maxwell
"The Estates of Christ" in
THEOLOGICAL PERSPECTIVES,
Edited by Paul R. Fetters
Copyright © 1992
by The Church of the United Brethren
in Christ

Whose News in an Open Field?
Can You Hear the Angel Band?
What is Your Christmas Attitude?
Who Rolled Away the Stone?
The Tomb is Empty! What of the Throne?
Who First Witnessed the Resurrection?
Who Saw Him First?

WHOSE NEWS IN AN OPEN FIELD?

Read: Luke 2:8-14

My wife Retha and I were gazing on the site for the second time. The first time, in 1985, we stood amazed and looked out over the same expansive flat area outside of modern Bethlehem in Israel. The field was much greener then than this time and the sky was clearer, lit with brighter stars, for we had been there in the month of June. This occurrence was in November. But the spectacle was the same. The Shepherds' Field, located three miles east of the town, stirred some of the same overwhelming responses in my heart that I sensed the first time.

The words recorded in the written record of Luke do not localize the exact place where the shepherds were that eventful night when the lead angel gave them the announcement of the Savior's birth. However, this site east of Bethlehem, more naturally than any other place nearby, fits the requirements necessary for a shepherd band and a field of sheep with an open sky expansive enough to entertain the whole multitude of the heavenly host which gave glory to God that night and their promise of peace. All of us in the tour group felt the strange pull of Christmas—even in early November! There can be very little reason to question why the ancient tradition has fixed this spot as the place the shepherds first heard the announcement of Jesus' birth. It truly is a natural!

Thirty-six of us, all believers, and our Jewess guide, remembered once again the age-old story of the angels appearing in the night sky to a group of lowly shepherds. We united to sing with new meaning some of the well-known Christmas songs, knowing full well that some of the lines did not express quite properly the actual facts surrounding the birth of our Savior. We, of course, do not know at all that it was "a cold winter night that was so deep" when Christ was born. The words of the beloved Christmas hymn, "Silent night, holy night; all is calm, all is bright," probably do not accurately express the atmosphere of those days and hours preceding and following this momentous event. The setting was anything but "silent" and "calm." There was a lot of hurried activity amidst the confusion of all the comings and goings in Bethlehem, for Caesar Augustus had issued a decree that a census should be taken of the entire Roman world, no doubt for tax purposes.

Joseph and Mary had come from Nazareth in Galilee and became a part of the swelling crowds which converged on Bethlehem to register because he belonged to the family of David. The scurrying and noise surely vented in raucous behavior on the part of many. I simply cannot imagine many of the people being happy to pay more taxes to Rome. Much less could I conceive of anyone present that night in Bethlehem saying of that bustling town, "How still we see thee lie." We know that the mass of people was so great that there was no room for the couple at any inn in the town. They may not at all have been the only ones lodging in the stable during those days.

Into these congested surroundings the Christ Child was born! I doubt seriously that the scene was so much under control that when the lowing of the cattle awakened Him, "no crying He (made)." There can be little doubt that the activities continued long into the night following the birth of this holy baby. So when the angels appeared in the open skies over the area where we were standing on this tour occasion, the town of Bethlehem three miles away continued its busy night time functions oblivious of what was transpiring in the shepherds' field. Why did not the appearance of angelic beings which filled the sky such a short distance away attract any attention in the town itself? We do not read anywhere in Luke's account that anyone in the town of Bethlehem itself even partially noticed anything unusual about the skies surrounding any part of the entire area!

What *is* written centers on these humble shepherds who were keeping a close watch over their sheep in this very area where we were standing. I was privileged to stand in front of a shepherd's grotto and read what Luke wrote: "And there were shepherds living out in the fields nearby, keeping watch over their flocks at night. An angel of the Lord appeared to them, and the glory of the Lord shone around them, and they were terrified. But the angel said to them, 'Do not be afraid. I bring you good news of great joy that will be for all people. Today in the town of David a Savior has been born to you; he is Christ the Lord...'" (Luke 2:8-11).

What full joy I sensed to be able to stand on that spot once again with my wife and experience the grip of the very place where the Heavenly Father chose over nineteen hundred years ago to make His heavenly announcement of the incarnate birth of His Son, our Messiah! Let's declare once again with that angel band of long ago: "Glory to God in the highest, and on earth peace to men on whom his favor rests" (Luke 2:14).

CAN YOU HEAR THE ANGEL BAND?

Read: Luke 2:8-20

"Suddenly a great company of the heavenly host appeared with the angel, praising God and saying, 'Glory to God in the highest and on earth peace to men on whom His favor rests,'" (Luke 2:13). It would have been exciting—and frightening—to have been with those lowly shepherds on that memorable evening when Christ was born. It would have been unbelievable to have heard that angelic music! I know that Luke does not expressly state that the angels "sang"—but I like to think they did! I choose to believe that the anthem swelled the heavens, beautiful and exhilarating, full of glory and resounding in power! Can you hear it now?

Upon the birth of a child in the holy land during the days of Caesar Augustus, the common practice was to conduct a musical celebration. Local musicians would come to stand outside the house of the parents of the newborn babe and play "welcoming music." Mirth and congratulations would mark the occasion, and a blessing would be offered.

Mary and Joseph, strangers in Bethlehem and seventy miles from home, held no expectations for such congenial visitors. Housed in the stable of an inn, these new parents of the Christ Child would not enjoy the company of musicians or their instruments—no singing, no public celebration. None would bring such welcome music to their new baby boy, for no one in the town of Bethlehem had any reason to know His birth date had arrived.

God in heaven, however, held other plans! He himself would send His own official "welcome musicians"—an angel band—to celebrate the birth of His son! One angel, commissioned to make the original announcement, would precede the anthem. A whole choir, consisting of a great company of the angelic hosts of heaven, would glorify God with "welcome music" from the skies!

To whom would the announcement of this celebration be offered? Not to the prophets, who had in fact predicted its certainty. Not to the scribes, who had transcribed the promises of this event and studied them with anticipation. Not to the priests, who had endeavored to explain those promises and had displayed their meanings through the sacrifices. These would not be the recipients of this joyful news.

The receivers would be lowly shepherds, the most common of all laborers of that day. They lived in the fields with their sheep and were among the least on the social scale. They were shunned by the orthodox religionists for they were viewed as unable to understand the meanings and blessings of synagogue worship. These shepherds cared for the very sheep, however, which were sacrificed in worship in the temple of Jerusalem. Could it be that these simple shepherds had come to understand more than the priests who offered the sacrifices? All we know for certain is that no one besides these humble shepherds would be privileged to hear the "welcome music" rendered by the angel band on that unforgettable night.

The message of music drove the joyful audience to action! Hurrying off, they found the Babe. And after they saw Him, they spread the word concerning what they had been told about this child.

None of us, obviously, was privileged to hear that great celebration presentation either. But the words which rolled across the heavens that evening have been recorded for all posterity. Now the whole world can hear! Can you hear the angel band again? "Glory to God in the highest, and on earth peace to men on whom

His favor rests!" Listen carefully! Let us hear those words again! Let their message, as with those shepherds of a former day, drive us to the action of sharing the heavenly news of great joy with renewed vigor and praise! Christ the Savior is born!

WHAT IS YOUR CHRISTMAS ATTITUDE?

Read: Philippians 2:5-11

We read in Philippians 2:5-11 that Jesus Christ was "in very nature God," and again, He "did not consider equality with God something to be grasped." This last assertion may warrant one of two meanings. It may mean that Christ did not have to "grasp" or "snatch at" equality with God, because He already possessed it as his right. Or it could mean He did not clutch at such equality as if to "hug it jealously to his breast." In either case we observe a word picture of Jesus that describes his former exalted position: "In the very form of God," "equal with God," and "one with God!"

With that tremendous description of Christ's preincarnate heavenly position, let's switch our focus to His earthly condescension where His selfless attitude emerges. The description of His former position greatly enhances what Paul states regarding His mindset on earth: "But made himself nothing, taking the very nature of a man...." The words "made himself nothing," embrace the idea of pouring out until nothing is left, to empty completely. So literally, "He emptied himself, taking the very nature of a man...."

Let's not misinterpret this statement, on the other hand, by pressing it too far. Of what did Jesus empty Himself? His deity? No! His sinlessness? Never! His perfection? Not at all! While fully maintaining His deity, as well as His sinlessness and perfection, He emptied Himself of His heavenly position and the reputation, the glory, and the freedom of His heavenly state. He had never been hampered by the confines of flesh and bone. He had never experienced the possibilities of pain, the pangs of sorrow or loneliness, or of weariness and temptation! In obedience to the everlasting plan of God, He took on Himself all of this willingly.

Beyond this, He emptied Himself of His right of rulership. He who formerly had maintained the eternal right to be served by legions of angels, emptied Himself of that special privilege and took on Himself "the very nature of a man"—was "made in human likeness." Through the mystery of the incarnation, the second person of the Godhead became a man! He did not cease to be God, but He did truly become man! He took the long step down from the heavenly to the earthly, fully identifying with mankind, being born of the virgin Mary. We celebrate that humble birth at Christmastime.

Was His willingness to become a man, then representative of the full extent of His consent to empty Himself? In no way! It was only the beginning! As a man, "He humbled Himself." To what extent? To "obedience." What kind of obedience? He was "obedient to death." What type of death? "Even death on a cross!" When Christ consented to death, He embraced mortality. When He subscribed to the cross He stooped to utter ignomy, for crucifixion in Christ's day was the most loathsome death possible. It was reserved for the lowest of criminals as an emblem of utter shame and reproach.

This attitude of utter yieldedness on the part of Christ sets the example for us who would follow Him. Paul's words challenge us. "Your attitude should be the same as that of Christ Jesus" (Philippians 2:5a). If the eternal Christ was willing for such self-emptying, His followers ought to have the same yieldedness toward God. We must be willing to weigh His will beside our will. At every juncture where these two conflict, we must say "yes" to His will and "no" to our will. Here is the essence of the attitude of Christ.

Say it often in the quiet, honesty of your inner soul, "I yield my all to Him, gladly and sincerely!" There is no more noble, Christlike Christmas attitude on the part of His followers than this!

WHO ROLLED AWAY THE STONE?

Read: Mark 16:1-8

No single event has changed the course of history like the resurrection of Jesus Christ! The empty tomb has persistently taunted the skeptical minds of would-be mockers through the centuries, and still challenges the reputed "enlightenment" of our present generation. There are now no viable arguments offered endeavoring to prove that the tomb of Jesus was not empty. The skeptic, the atheist, the believer and agnostic have all come to "agreement" that the tomb, by all known historical facts, did, in fact, become empty. The arguments center solely on *how* the tomb became empty.

English journalist Frank Morison, a number of years ago, set out to write a book designed to prove that Christ could not have actually emerged alive from the grave. He explored at length the arguments others had already proposed. The more deeply he delved into the pros and cons of those proposals, and the more intense his personal honesty became as he grappled with his own theories, the more persistently one question insisted upon surfacing to plague his mind: "Who moved the stone?" He knew that the stone, sealed in place over the opening, would certainly have to have been rolled back in order for anyone to enter or for Jesus to exit. But he also knew that stone was large (some, whether correctly or not, have estimated it to be a solid wheel of granite, eight feet in diameter and at least one foot thick and weighing more than four tons). Suppose it weighed only three tons! What would change? Among all of those who were to have played parts in the various theories of explaining why the tomb was empty, who could qualify to have rolled the stone away from the opening?

Could it have been *the women*? Not a chance! One of the questions asked among themselves on their way to visit the tomb on that memorable morning was, "Who will roll the stone away from the entrance of the tomb?" (Mark 16:3) It was obvious to them that they would never be able to perform that task. Nor could one man perform such a feat on his own, ruling out *the gardener* (a very few have suggested he removed the body to keep curiosity seekers away). And would it not certainly dispense with the theory that *Jesus Himself* moved the stone? There are those who assert that Jesus did not really die but instead went into a near death state of unconsciousness resulting from His wounds, only to revive and, in spite of His weakened state, push aside the stone from the inside! Impossible! Besides, whether trying to enter the tomb or exit, both of these men would have had to encounter the guards assigned to hinder either.

What of *Joseph of Arimathea*? Could he not have, for some reason changed his mind and enlisted help to remove the body of Jesus from his own personal tomb to a more permanent resting place? Possibly. But it must have been done under one of two circumstances—either with the permission of the Jewish authorities, or in clandestine secrecy. If performed under the former circumstance, the Jewish authorities would have had full knowledge, solving a lot of problems later when the disciples were declaring the resurrection! How, on the other hand, could it have been done under the second circumstance? Do we really think that Joseph would have finally declared himself openly a believer in Jesus, even following His death, and willingly incurred the contempt of his old Jewish associates and the hostility of the priesthood (as apocryphal literature definitely indicates), only to part from it all within 36 hours? I can't buy that! But if he had, what of the guard again? Why would the assigned temple guard have not either hindered him or reported him to the Jewish authorities who were already angry with him? This, of course, did not happen.

Is it possible *the Jewish authorities* (with or without the help of

Joseph), or even *the Roman authorities*, enlisted the very help of the assigned guards to remove the body? They could have. But why? After all, they did not want the people to believe the body was gone. Their guards had been assigned to keep the body there! Of course, if either had removed the body, they would have known where the ultimate and final resting place was. In that case, neither the Jews nor the Romans would have been content to hear the disciples declare openly a few weeks later His resurrection without producing the body! In one stroke they could have destroyed forever the message of his physical resurrection—but this, strangely, was not forthcoming!

Could *the disciples* have moved the stone? The sacred record tells us that some members of the guard reported that this was, in fact, what happened while they slept. This meant, obviously, that eleven frightened disciples had slipped between the guard personnel, rolled that enormous stone aside and those guards could witness to all that transpired, though every one of them had slept through the entire incident! Sorry, my sense of better judgement cannot embrace that! Mr. Morison also struggled with such proposals. Finally he concluded his study by writing a book entitled, *WHO MOVED THE STONE?* (now published by Lamplighter Books), a strong searching investigation into the scriptural story of the death of Christ, establishing the unquestionable point that the resurrection was a genuine historical fact.

Who rolled the stone away indeed? The Scripture tells us that "an angel of the Lord came down from heaven and, going to the tomb, rolled back the stone and sat on it" (Matthew 28:2). He did this, not so much to let Jesus out, but to let those on the outside in that they could witness His already completed triumph over death! And He lives today! Let us proclaim it with highest confidence. He lives! And because He lives, we too, shall live!

THE TOMB IS EMPTY! WHAT OF THE THRONE?

Read: Matthew 28:1-7

In June 1985, my wife and I enjoyed the privilege of standing before the opening of the Garden Tomb just outside the city walls of Jerusalem. The memory of that occasion seems like last week. I will never forget the sense of awe and unworthiness I felt as I realized this could well be the very place where the body of our Savior lay following His crucifixion. As we entered the tomb, no one spoke. Every person in our group worshipped the risen Christ in hushed silence and with a sense of renewed consecration to our Lord who is alive! When we emerged, I saw only one who was not weeping. We visited the site a second time in November 1996. This time she and I stood together—just the two of us—to worship!

I am very much aware of the difficulty attempting to prove that this Garden Tomb site is actually the very place the body of Christ lay (though it does seem to fulfill every detail of the description given in the Gospel record). Years ago a hired guide at the Garden Tomb, who was a Spirit-filled Christian, used to give a Gospel message about the resurrection to groups he led through the garden site. Those groups would consist of many believers. But periodically, agnostics as well as atheists, all obviously skeptical, also would be present. His presentation would reach a crescendo as he stood in front of the open tomb and, with one hand toward heaven, triumphantly declare, "The tomb is empty, but the throne is filled! The tomb is empty, but the throne is filled!"

One day a member of a touring group taunted him: "Sir, you know full well there is another site in the city which one whole segment of Christianity believes is the place where Jesus was buried. It certainly cannot be both places, can it? There is no way you can be absolutely certain that this is the place!" Without blinking, the guide retorted emphatically, "And, sir, I remind you that *both* tombs are empty, but the throne is filled! *Both* tombs are empty but the throne is filled!"

Blinking back tears, I remember saying to myself on that first visit as I stood with the other worshippers inside the tomb, "This could very well be the place! If it is not, the place where Jesus lay was very much like this one and very near this spot!"

The final issue for us does not center in the *place*. The issue centers in the *person*. Nearly two thousand years ago, our Savior, the Lord Jesus Christ, was nailed to a cross for your sins and mine. They placed His body in a tomb which was located just outside the walls of Jerusalem near a hill called "the place of the skull." A mammoth, round stone, cut flat, was put to use to cover the tomb entrance. It was rolled into place on its gulley shaped track and fixed with a Roman seal. Armed soldiers, probably about sixteen strong, assigned by the authorities of Jerusalem, stood guard lest anyone should come to steal the body.

But God the Father, as He has always been prone to do, put in motion other plans! On Sunday morning, following the Sabbath, He raised Christ, His Son, from the dead! Jesus came out of the tomb alive forever more! To assure His followers that Jesus lives again, the Father sent an angel from heaven to break the seal and roll the large stone away, declaring to those who came to the tomb, "He is not here. He is risen! Come, see the place where the Lord lay!"

The fact that He who was dead is now alive is the triumphant note of Easter! The fact that He has truly conquered death is the basis for our faith in Him! We can well afford to believe that He gives us new life here and now, and will some day raise our bodies from death in the power of the resurrection.

The tomb is truly empty! But your heart need not be empty.
Let the risen Christ make your heart His throne—and celebrate
His eternal life in the power of His resurrection. The tomb is empty,
but the throne is filled!

WHO FIRST WITNESSED THE RESURRECTION?

Read: Matthew 28:4, 11-15

We sometimes overlook the fact that the first human beings to bear public witness to the resurrection of Jesus Christ were not His friends. They were His enemies—some of the appointed solders who were in the armed guard to watch the tomb.

We read that "some of the guards went into the city and reported to the chief priests everything that had happened" (Matthew 28:11). I presume they would have known the truth whereof they spoke, for they were there when it all happened. They witnessed the lightning-like angel, dressed in white, descending from the heavens with the violent shaking of an earthquake. They saw him roll the stone away. Trembling with fear, they became as dead men (Matthew 28:4).

Now let us understand that these soldiers would have been the last people on earth to benefit by telling their story. Punishment for failing while on guard duty was death. What would prompt them, in the face of such punitive threat, to go before the Jewish authorities and tell everything that had happened? We may rest assured they never would have made such a bizarre confession unless the allegations to which they bore witness were true.

We may conclude, as well, that the chief priests were convinced by what the soldiers said—so much so, that instead of reporting them to the Roman authorities to be punished, they contrived a story to cover the facts and persuaded the soldiers to cooperate at a large price of bribe money. And what was that story? The elders instructed them, "You are to say, 'His disciples came during the night and stole him away while we were asleep.' If this report gets to the governor, we will satisfy him and keep you out of trouble" (Matthew 28:13,14). And that story went out among the people.

Of course, what the authorities were asking of those who heard that report, and of us today, is that they and we be willing to believe that eleven fearful men with two swords among them (Luke 22:38) mustered enough courage to face the sixteen or more well-armed soldiers who formed the guard! We are to believe that when they arrived at the tomb, every one of those soldiers was fast asleep—and that, on the very day it was said Jesus would rise! We are to believe, further, that these eleven would-be grave robbers slipped between those sleeping soldiers, broke the seal, rolled that mammoth stone (which might have weighed four tons) aside, entered the tomb, snatched the body of Jesus, exited, made their way back between those sleeping guards, and scored a clean getaway—and not one of those men was awakened! Of course, they are asking us to believe some of the guards could testify with integrity to all of this though they were fast asleep when it happened! Only a fool could accept such an incredible piece of fiction!

Bribe money altered the public testimony of these soldiers, but that money could never change the facts! Let's not forget, that before these men spread their incredible story of grave-robbing by the disciples, they had freely and spontaneously confessed to what had actually happened! In so doing, they became the first human witnesses to the true account of the resurrection of our Lord and Savior, Jesus Christ!

Let these facts reaffirm to our hearts the glorious good news of the power of Christ over death! He is risen indeed! And He lives forevermore!

WHO SAW HIM FIRST?

Read: John 20:10-18

The first believers to see Jesus alive following His resurrection were not the men who had been with Him from the beginning of His ministry. Those who saw Him first were some of the women. The *very* first was Mary Magdalene. Let's follow Mary on that memorable morning as she learned of the greatest event history has ever witnessed.

She and the other women had prepared to perform a common practice of that day when death occurred by making ready spices to anoint Jesus' body. Arriving at the tomb early in the morning, they were shocked to find the large stone already rolled away from the mouth of the grave!

SEEING THE STONE, MARY WITHDREW. While the others entered the tomb, John records that Mary wheeled around and ran back to the sorrowing disciples and excitedly blurted out, "They have taken the Lord out of the tomb and we don't know where they put him!" (John 20:1-2) Her motive was right. Her message was wrong! Had she not reacted so quickly, she would have heard the angel say to the other women, "Be not afraid. You seek Jesus of Nazareth who was crucified. He is risen, he is not here" (Mark 16:6).

Shall we fault Mary at this point? I don't think so! Have we not also jumped to hasty conclusions at times which, though sincere, have been wrong? If we would stop in our reactionary haste, we might also hear his message in our traumatic circumstances. We, like Mary, have also missed the message of angels and run with our own sincere, but wrong, report!

Peter and John, upon hearing Mary's message, immediately ran to the tomb. Mary followed, and when the men had left the site, she remained.

SEEING THE SEPULCHER, MARY WEPT. Her tears were so genuine! They were also completely unnecessary! Mary, like many of us, did not realize that the traumatic cause for her weeping had already been remedied! She was standing in the very presence of Christ's victory and could not embrace it! Through her tears she bent over and looked into the tomb and saw two angels in white. "Woman, why are you crying?" they asked.

"They have taken my Lord away," was her hopeless reply, "and I don't know where they have put him." Obviously she did not recognize these beings to be angels.

Turning, she saw one whom she thought to be the gardener. "Sir, if you have carried him away, tell me where you have put him, and I will get him."

At this desperate moment in her attempt to understand what was happening, Jesus spoke her name! "Mary." Can you imagine, the utter shock Mary felt the moment she recognized Jesus? The joy! He was alive again after all! She saw him for herself— and her reaction was spontaneous! Reaching out to embrace her Lord, her cry could be heard throughout the garden area: "Rabboni (Teacher)!" (John 20:16)

The reply of Jesus was as sensitive and tender as it was direct: "Do not hold on to me, for I have not yet returned to the Father" (John 20:17).

SEEING THE SAVIOR, MARY WORSHIPPED. Her unconstrained response at seeing Jesus was, in fact, worship! You and I now have the privilege, by an eye of faith, to also see our risen Lord for ourselves! The Hebrew writer declares, "At present we do not see everything put under him. But we see Jesus...now crowned with glory and honor...!" (Hebrews 2:8-9). By such an eye of faith, can you see Him now?

Jesus said to Mary, "Go to my brothers and tell them..." (John 20:17). And Mary set out to return to the disciples, who at this point, with the possible exception of John (John 20:8), were still a skeptical lot!

SEEING THE SKEPTICS, MARY WITNESSED. She apparently arrived about the same time as did the other women who had been at the tomb. Her message: "I have seen the Lord!" (John 20:18). She told them that He had said all these things to her.

Do we not rub shoulders continually with people who have never been able to exercise enough faith to see the risen Lord? Shall not we, who by faith have seen the Lord, like Mary, share that revelation of the power of the resurrection with those who still have trouble believing? Let us declare to all with new fervor and conviction, "He is alive! I have seen the Lord! He lives in my heart!"

MEASURING OUR DAYS

"What you do with your time is a reflection of your values and priorities..Doing the right thing is to be settled before doing things right! To think through what are the right things to do before worrying about the right way to do them will save us from hours of wasted energy!"

Brian W. Livermore
Stated in "Mastering Your Time"
Correspondence Course
Trinity College & Theological Seminary
Newburg, Indiana

Are We Numbering Our Days?
How Much Time Do We Need?
Will You "Live" All the Rest of Your Life?
How About Living and Dying?
Can One Still Speak When Time Runs Out?
Do You Still Believe Jesus is Coming Soon?
Are You Anticipating His Coming?

ARE WE NUMBERING OUR DAYS?

Read: Psalm 39:4-5; 90:12

Have you become aware that whenever we enter a new year, or celebrate another birthday, or face some crisis, we tend to evaluate time more carefully than we normally do otherwise? We become more conscious of just how quickly time is slipping by. We take a closer, and more discriminating, look at the way we have put our time to use to that point. We think more seriously of "numbering our days."

As born-again Christians, we must often remind ourselves of the precious quality of the time God has given us, and will offer in the future. I was shocked the first time I realized that a fifteen minute coffee break twice a day, five days a week, amounts to a full three-week vacation by the end of a year! I could hardly believe that over a forty year working life, a person could spend nearly two and one-half years on break drinking coffee!

I still find it difficult to imagine that if one lives to the age of seventy and experiences quite a normal life, he or she will spend nearly twenty years sleeping! More than twenty years working! And almost six years eating! Not quite seven years will be piddled away playing—and fully five years dressing! Probably about a full year will be invested simply talking on the telephone (for some much more)! About three years will be spent waiting for someone, and at least two years on vacation! Here is the shocker: only one and a half years will be spent in church!—that is, if the person is a *regular attender*. No wonder the great Bible expositor, John Stott, nearing the end of his third lecture at an Inter-Varsity Christian Fellowship missionary convention, begged the congregation,

"Please don't clap any more; you're wasting my time! I've only got two minutes more!" Time drives a hard bargain! With a strong desire not to allow the rest of our lives to "just happen," and with a purpose to "number our days that we may apply our heart to wisdom," we ought to ask ourselves two very important questions. The first is this: *"What is my real purpose in life?"* Is my purpose for my life clear to me? A purpose constitutes a general aim, pointing us in the direction of achieving things which are designed to *shape* our future. One of the most valuable and searching exercises I ever experienced was to sit down and write out my own personal purpose statement. If you have never done so, I strongly suggest that you take the two or three hours necessary to do so. They could prove to be some of the most important hours of your life!

The second question we should ask ourselves is this: *"What are my specific goals for my immediate future and beyond?"* A goal is a statement about a proposed future accomplishment which is measurable and puts meat on the bones of one's purpose statement. Goals place sign posts to tell us how far we have come. For you "old-timer" baseball fans, it was Yogi Berra who said, "If you don't know where you're going, you'll probably end up somewhere else!" He is also the sage who, regarding the necessity of making important decisions in life, said, "If you come to a fork in the road—take it!"

One of two measurable goals in each of the following areas will help one to keep clearly focused: *spiritual goals*, relating to growth in faith and worship; *mental goals* related to learning; *physical goals* relating to health and well-being; *social goals* relating to friends and neighbors; *family goals* relating to relationships; *vocational goals* relating to achievement and work; *financial goals* relating to saving, spending and sharing; *personal goals* relating to hobbies and enjoyment; and *retirement goals*, relating to productive senior life.

Here are some proven guidelines for setting worthy goals:

1. *A goal should be written and specific*, forcing us to think through its real essence and enabling us to measure the progress being made.

2. *A goal should be personal and desirable.* We should ask, "What does this goal really mean to me? What do I really want to accomplish in the long run?"

3. *A goal should be challenging and accomplishable.* It must inspire us and be attainable, consistent with our gifts and abilities.

4. *A goal should be consistent, while flexible.* It should be compatible with our purpose statement as well as with our other goals. We must be willing, however, to refine, review and update when necessary.

The prospects of the future to a Bible Christian are extremely challenging. Let the prayer of the Psalmist be our heart cry as we embrace its possibilities and hopes: "So teach us to number our days, that we may apply our hearts unto wisdom" (Psalm 90:12).

HOW MUCH TIME DO WE NEED?

Read: Ephesians 5:15-16

"I just don't have enough time!" Sound familiar? Who of us has never felt such frustration?

The apostle Paul placed high value on our time. "Be very careful how you live," he wrote, "not as unwise but as wise, making the most of every opportunity because the days are evil" (Ephesians 5:15,16). His goal is not that we as believers all become "time nuts." He does, however, remind us that we must take very seriously the fact that we will be held accountable for our use of the time God has given us. It was Ben Franklin who said, "Dost thou love life? Then do not squander time, for that's the stuff life is made of!"

I believe three facts must challenge us anew as we evaluate the amount of time we Christians will invest in various and sundry pursuits during the remainder of our lives. *The first is this: We all have essentially the same amount of time, 24 hours each day, no more, no less!* Someone has written, "Yesterday is a cancelled check. Tomorrow is a promissory note. Today is the only cash we have—so spend it wisely." The fact is, we do not need more time. Rather, we need to make much better use of the time we have.

The proper use of our time, then, becomes to us a major issue of prioritizing. Three questions force themselves upon our discriminatory powers of selection in the setting of these priorities. First, "Of all the possible ways we have at our disposal to invest our time, which are truly the most important?" Again, "How much of what we consider to be important does God actually consider valuable in the light of eternity?" Finally, "Recognizing that we can make decisions only during that segment of time called 'now'— but also recognizing that our long view always tends to sharpen our short view—how far into the future shall we look when making those present decisions which will greatly affect that future?"

The second fact which has to be important to us is this: To be in control of our time, we must be in control of ourselves! To bring ourselves under control, we must confront head-on our deeply entrenched routines. Long standing habits become extremely calloused and unresponsive to the challenge of higher priorities! They are difficult to break. New and more positive ones are even more difficult to establish. It will certainly necessitate the enablement of the indwelling Holy Spirit. So to truly exercise self-control, we must willingly place ourselves under the complete control of the Holy Spirit. "You...are not controlled by the sinful nature but by the Spirit, if the Spirit of God lives in you" (Romans 8:8,9).

So *time*-management in our lives becomes *life*-management. It must be practiced and developed all the days of our lives, one day at a time. It must become a daily discipline as each day is recognized as a fresh opportunity to begin anew to formulate better habits involving the use of our time. This practice will become increasingly focused as we place in highest priority those practices which are most important to fulfilling God's plan and purpose for our lives.

The third fact of importance is this: Direction is more important than speed. We live in a day of computers, fast foods, quick fixes and speedy travel. We are programmed toward immediate, high tech results. We will probably find it difficult to keep aware of the fact that the object of "making the best use our time" is not necessarily to "get as much done as possible in the fewest possible moments." In fact, it is quite possible for any of us to accomplish many tasks, the majority of which do not really matter. God is much more concerned that we select the most important of all the possible tasks available, which will most effectively fulfill His purpose for our lives, and do them to the best degree we are able.

I wish I could give credit to the author of the following lines. He or she is unknown to me, but wraps up my thoughts on this subject rather succinctly: "This is the beginning of a new day. God has given me this day to use as I will. I can waste it, or use it for good. What I do today is very important because I am exchanging a day of my life for it. When tomorrow comes, this day will be gone forever, leaving something in its place I have traded for it. I want it to be gain, not loss—good, not evil—success, not failure—in order that I shall not forget the price I paid for it." Amen!

WILL YOU "LIVE" ALL THE REST OF YOUR LIFE?

Read: Philippians 1:19-26

More than 25 years ago my wife Retha and I sat in the living room of the parsonage of the West Eckford Missionary Church in Marshall, Michigan. Doctors had just discovered that she had cancer. Through tears, we evaluated and discussed more realistically than we ever had before what living and dying really meant to us. We talked of heaven and how our hope beyond the grave affected what we were facing.

Retha, after a number of such sessions was finally able to settle one matter. "I don't know how long I will live," she concluded, "but I choose to 'die' only once. As God helps me, I am going to truly 'live' all the rest of my life!" God was very merciful and, through surgery and radiation, touched and healed her body. I can testify on her behalf that she has been and is truly "living" the rest of her life. We give to God the praise!

It is quite apparent that long before the apostle Paul experienced imprisonment and the very real threat of death for preaching Christ, he had fully appraised what both living and dying meant to him. In Philippians 1:21 (written from prison), he expresses these feelings in two sweeping statements of faith, one depicting his evaluation of life, the other of death.

In his assessment of life, Paul speaks to the very heart and soul of the greatest dilemma many people encounter. They have never come to understand the marked difference between "being alive" and "living."

Ben Robertson, in his book, **RED HILLS AND COTTON**, tells of a tombstone near his boyhood home on which are inscribed the following words: "Born 1810. Died 1890. Lived 50 years."

George Bernard Shaw as an old man resentfully complained, "Life is a disease." He further concluded that the epitaph most appropriate for many people might read, "Died at thirty. Buried at sixty." What a tragic mindset!

Even as he penned the Philippian writing, Paul was a prisoner of the Roman government—a government which had all of the power necessary to have him executed for his beliefs in Jesus Christ. During his approximately two year waiting period spent chained to a Roman guard, he had much time to assess carefully what life really meant to him, and what the reality of dying would mean to him. His conclusions? First of all, concerning life, he boils it down to its very basic ingredient: "For to me, to live is Christ!" That's it! Does it sound simplistic? Ah no! It is profound! He asserts that everything which makes life worth living—truly complete, rich, significant, full—is found in Jesus Christ! To enter and maintain a very personal relationship with this Christ, to Paul, formed the very core and fiber of everything that made up life.

And what then of death? He says in the same verse, "...and to die is gain!" That embraces eternal gain!

A few short years ago I sat at the bedside of a brother-in-law just days before he passed into the presence of Jesus. His life had clearly demonstrated his Spirit-filled relationship with Christ. Now he was about to face the reality of dying. Though he was semiconscious most of the time, when I read to him the Word of God and prayed, his eyes opened. He clearly articulated his appreciation for other verses which he had underlined in his Bible. He asked me to read some of those verses, too. The hope beyond the grave was so very real to him!

John Wesley used to say to those who criticized the brand of religion he preached, "But our people die well!" D. L. Moody, famous American evangelist, spoke exultantly to a group of friends: "Some morning you will read in the papers that D. L. Moody is dead. Don't believe a word of it! At that moment, I shall be more alive than I am now. I was born in the flesh in 1837. I was born of the Spirit in 1856. That which is born of the flesh may die; that which is born of the Spirit shall live forever!" That is eternal gain!

Let us not allow life to shortchange us. Let us not allow the prospect of death to shackle us with fear and doubt. We too, can find that to truly live is to experience "Christ in us," and to die is to "be present with the Lord." To the biblical Christian, whether living or dying, we win!

HOW ABOUT LIVING AND DYING?

Read: Romans 4:7-9

We believe that genuine salvation in Jesus Christ adequately prepares one for both complete living and triumphant dying. Paul Fretz, former associate director with World Partners, the overseas arm of the Missionary Church denomination of the U.S. and the Evangelical Missionary Church of Canada, epitomized both aspects of this fact in grand fashion! Those of us who knew him best knew well that he loved his Savior, and we watched him live out his life to the full in the will of God. On May 23, 1992, following a six-week siege of fighting for his life in an Ontario, California hospital, he died the death of one who was triumphant in Jesus. Some of us, even after these number of years, still find it difficult to accept that one so full of life and energy, and so full of creative ways to support missions, is silenced by death. But it is so. It has caused us to contemplate anew the realities involved in living and dying.

I believe periodically every one of us ought to push aside all speculations of lesser importance and conduct a thorough evaluation of our innermost thoughts concerning the life we are living and the death we will die. We ought to face ourselves squarely with at least two very personal questions regarding our living. First, what do we honestly believe is the most important ingredient in life—more important than anything else? Second, are our lives truly demonstrating that what we profess as so important actually is that important to us?

I believe we also ought to ask ourselves at least four very personal questions about dying. First, with what assurances do we expect to die? Secondly, what do we really believe is involved in dying? Thirdly, what do we actually believe lies beyond death for us? And finally, are we truly inculcating into our lives those elements necessary to prepare us adequately for what we say we believe about death?

The world is so full of those who expend their entire lives refusing to come to terms with the fact that some day they will die. Their "loose cannon" attitudes camouflage any fleeting thoughts they might periodically entertain about "being ready to die." To outrun death is their greatest challenge in life!

Others are different. Their greatest problems do not center in death and dying. Their greatest concern is that they have never learned how to truly live! They seldom consider that life can be so much more than self centered pursuits—more than breathing and "making a living"—more than just "taking care of 'number one.'"

The apostle Paul, in his Roman letter, maintains that to the born again Christian, life must exceed just being alive and dogging the path of self-centered goals! Death is certainly more than simply "checking out!" Life can be worth every bit of all the living involved, and death can be everlasting "gain!" But such living and dying is possible only as we live and invest our lives very truly "for the Lord Jesus Christ." It is "living for the Lord" that makes "dying for the Lord" possible. Here is how the apostle expresses it: for the committed Christian, "none of us lives to himself alone and none of us dies to himself alone. If we live, we live to the Lord; and if we die, we die to the Lord. So, whether we live or die we belong to the Lord" (Romans 14:7-8).

It is the Lord alone, our Savior, Jesus Christ, Who puts a different light and brighter hue on both living and dying. How has He made this possible? For He himself faced and conquered both life and death. He lived a sinless life! He died a real death! He rose from the dead through the power of the resurrection! "For this

very reason," writes the author of Romans, "Christ died and returned to life so that He might be the Lord of both the dead and the
living" (Romans 14:9). He fills life with eternal meaning. And
He transforms death itself into eternal life!

What could be better? For all of us who are surely following
the path my friend Paul Fretz has taken, moving toward our appointment with death, let us be very certain that Jesus Christ is our
Lord—our all in all in our living! Then we shall also find, by
personal experience as he has, that when we die, we "die to the
Lord! So, whether we live or die, we belong to the Lord!" Thus,
living is full of meaning and dying is truly never ending gain!
Amen! So be it!

CAN ONE STILL SPEAK WHEN TIME RUNS OUT?

Read: Hebrews 11:4

I first came under the influence of Richard Reilly's ministry in the late 1940s. I was one of the pre-teen guys who attended the Saturday night Youth for Christ rallies in Elkhart, Indiana. Dick (as he was better known) was the YFC director in Elkhart. Little did I realize then how much this local YFC director would touch my life with a missionary vision that would shape a good share of my service in Nigeria, West Africa, in later years.

Dick never tired of relating how he, as a teenaged newsboy, and a member of a Detroit street gang, stepped into a storefront chapel one wet evening to escape the rain. What he heard intrigued him, and that night he gave his heart to Christ and left that chapel a redeemed child of God. That spiritual conversion to the Lord Jesus completely changed his life.

Conducive to his nature, the next few years moved by quickly. Bible college and seminary followed his conversion. In 1942 he married and entered the ministry. Three years later he was ordained in the Missionary Church, and that same year accepted his appointment to the directorship of Youth for Christ in Elkhart.

God's plan for Dick not only included YFC. He also became a pastor—then a missionary to India—and later was selected as the Foreign Secretary of the United Missionary Society, where he served until 1969. Following a brief term as a missionary to Lebanon, he served as an evangelist with the Missionary Church and later became the founder and president of two Christian travel agencies. Over his lifetime he flew more than 2½ million miles on commercial airlines visiting 87 countries as a missionary executive or travel agent. Considered an excellent and forceful communicator, he was well-known among congregations in the U.S. and Canada for his unique multimedia prophecy conferences which became a favorite among the major portion of those who heard him.

Hundreds of participants greatly profited from his tours to major destinations of the world, including numerous times to Israel, Jordan, Egypt, Rome and Athens. He visited the Holy Land more than 300 times and became recognized as one of the most knowledgeable authorities on its history and archeological discoveries.

It was while Dick was the Foreign Secretary of the United Missionary Society that his missionary passion gripped my own life in a lasting way. I expressed something of my appreciation to him for that influence in a letter dated August 6, 1992 in which I wrote, "I want to thank you, Dick, for allowing God to use you to breathe into my heart a passion for missions years ago. The seminar you conducted for outgoing missionaries before Retha and I went to Nigeria shaped my whole basic attitude toward missions and our work in Nigeria. I thank God for that influence." His evident drive to reach unevangelized people and unreached people groups still strikes the rhythm chord of my present day heartbeat!

A massive stroke silenced Dick's earthly voice on February 24, 1994, at age 76, ushering him into the presence of the Savior he came to know so many years earlier in that storefront chapel. But the memory of his strong spirit and missionary vision still speaks to me and to many others of my era. He left behind, in fact, a whole host of positive memories for a lot of us who knew him which will, even though he is gone, continue to prod us on to an ever enlarging vision of the spiritual need of a whole hurting world! Time ran out—but he still speaks with a strong missionary voice today!

He "fought the good fight!" He "finished the race!" He "kept the faith!" He found, as has every faithful child of the Lord who has died in faith, that there was in store for him the crown of righteousness, which the Lord, the righteous Judge, will award to him on that day! Final reunion day is coming!

DO YOU STILL BELIEVE JESUS IS COMING SOON?

Read: Matthew 24:36-42

One of the priority teachings of the Bible which must govern our lives as Christians is that Jesus is coming again—soon! What happens, however, when someone's teaching presses beyond what the Scripture states?

Possibly you remember vividly back to 1987-88 how the attention of thousands of people was riveted on the prediction of Edgar C. Whisenant that Jesus Christ would return in the rapture between September 11-13, 1988. His book, 88 REASONS WHY THE RAPTURE WILL BE IN 1988, was purchased in bundles. Anticipation mounted and fear for some became evident as the final hour approached. In various quarters the work of evangelism took fire. Some repented as a result (for which I am truly grateful).

I remember clearly how semi-guilty I felt, however, when I shared with fellow Christians that I, as well as many others, could not espouse the growing euphoria. Jesus had made a statement recorded in Matthew 24:36 which kept torpedoing any excitement that I tried to muster. When the rotation of the earth on its axis finally ushered in September 14, great disappointment gripped the hearts of hundreds of sincere Christians. Why? Because they had chosen to ignore the full impact of the simple statement Jesus gave with such obvious clarity concerning that event: "No one knows about that day or hour, not even the angels in heaven, nor the Son (though the Son certainly knows *now* that He has gone back to Heaven), but only the Father...Therefore keep watch, because you do not know on what day your Lord will come" (Matthew 24:36, 42). The bare truth of that inspired statement somehow was lost in the shuffle of the exciting predictions! It was simply forgotten that not even Whisenant could know, notwithstanding his years of careful and logical study with all of its plausible conclusions. No man could know!

In spite of the excitement and the quickness of sincere Christians to "buy into" a prediction which pressed beyond what the Scripture claims, the cold fact of the bottom line is this—he was dead wrong! I remember asking myself, "What will be the fallout among disappointed Christians and frightened sinners? Only time will tell!" I thought that some of us would probably be picking up the pieces for a long time after that. Happily, that did not prove true. A few suffered great emotional disappointment, the most traumatic of which, I understand, came to Whisenant himself. But this was not widespread, thankfully. My greatest concern, however, was not whether sincere people would throw away their confidence that Jesus was going to come again. My concern was that something of the sharp anticipation "that His coming *could* be very soon" would simply be blunted and dulled in the hearts of many. I think my concerns, and that of others, at this point, were valid.

What can we learn from this experience? Several lessons emerge. First, we must always question the claims of anyone whose self-proclaimed revelations press beyond what the Scripture clearly teaches. Secondly, the disappointment in a false hope on the part of some ought never shake the confidence of those whose faith is firmly anchored in the true hope! Thirdly, since enough information is clearly revealed in the Bible that teaches the coming of Jesus is near, let us maintain spiritual readiness. Jesus said, "So you must also be ready, because the Son of Man will come at an hour when you do not expect him" (Matthew 24:44). Fourthly, if the suspicion that Christ might have come during September 11-13, 1988, could drive so many to sincere evangelism, should not the scriptural fact that His coming is near also prompt such action?

Finally, if a false expectation of Christ's return could ignite more careful living, ought not a sensible expectation founded firmly in the scriptures prompt us to the same, and even more so?

Let the closing statements of the New Testament encourage your heart as you continue to anticipate the coming of your Savior. Jesus said, "Yes, I am coming soon." And John's response should be ours: "Amen, Come, Lord Jesus."

ARE YOU ANTICIPATING HIS COMING?

Read: Acts 1:9-12

Luke states in Acts 1:12 that following Jesus' ascension back to the Father, the disciples "returned to Jerusalem from the hill called the Mount of Olives, a Sabbath day's walk from the city."

The Mount of Olives is situated on the east side of Jerusalem. The half-mile wide Kidron Valley separates the city from this sacred elevated spot where Jesus was prone to meet with His disciples for teaching and prayer. It stands 2,680 feet above sea level, which means it is about 200 feet higher than the temple area in the old city of Jerusalem (now under Muslim jurisdiction) located directly across the valley where the eastern wall and the Eastern Gate are in full view.

Down the mountain toward the Kidron Valley is located the Garden of Gethsemane where Jesus prayed during His last hours before His arrest. Here today stand some of the most ancient olive trees on earth, among which a few could possibly date back to Jesus' time. Some would claim with "guarded certainty" that it is believable that Jesus knelt under or near some of these very trees!

On the top of that mountain today stands the Chapel of the Ascension, an eight-sided building with a round dome which marks the traditional spot where Jesus ascended to heaven. Inside the chapel is the rock from which Jesus is purported (of course, not with unquestioned validity) to have been taken up from the earth to His Father. Whether or not this is truly the very rock from which Jesus ascended is not the issue. The issue is this: from this mountaintop Jesus did, in fact, ascend back to heaven!

Luke reports that Jesus "was taken up before their very eyes, and a cloud hid him from their sight. They were looking intently up into the sky as he was going, when suddenly two men dressed in white stood beside them. 'Men of Galilee,' they said, 'why do you stand here looking into the sky? This same Jesus, who has been taken from you into heaven will come back in the same way you have seen him go into heaven'" (Acts 1:9-11).

My wife and I were privileged some time ago to stand with Dr. Vernon Petersen, our tour leader, and thirty-three other believers on this very spot in the Chapel of the Ascension. I read the Scripture just quoted and made some pertinent comments, and one of the group, led us as we united to sing, "Jesus is Coming Again!" My heart felt something of the growing sense of anticipation which one experiences in that setting. It still beats faster when I recall the incident! A person cannot be in Israel long without becoming aware that, among dedicated Jews who still believe the Old Testament Scripture, there exists a growing expectancy that the time for their long promised Messiah to make His appearance is drawing near. What a shame that their forefathers missed recognizing that very appearance when He did, in fact, come to the world, born of a virgin and announced by angels.

He lived His sinless life among them. He died on the cross for their sins—and ours! He was buried in a tomb outside their city. He rose from the dead in mighty power on the third day—and, after forty days, ascended back to the Father.

Ah yes! Their Messiah—and ours—will surely make His appearance! And the time for that appearance is certainly drawing near! It will not be His first coming, however, but the final phase of His second coming! The prophet Zechariah declares that His feet will stand on this very spot again— "on the Mount of Olives, east of Jerusalem, and the Mount of Olives will be split in two from east to west, forming a great valley, with half the mountain moving north and half moving south...Then the Lord my God will come, and all the holy ones with him" (Zechariah 14:3-5).

What is our immediate concern as we anticipate the fulfillment of Zechariah's prediction? Let us be living in a state of readiness for the *first* phase of this coming, when the Lord Himself will come down from heaven "in a flash, in the twinkling of an eye..." (1 Corinthians 15:52). "The dead in Christ will rise first. After that, we who are still alive and are left will be caught up with them in the clouds to meet the Lord in the air. And so we will be with the Lord forever" (1 Thessalonians 4:16-17). Since the fact is established that from the time of the rapture on, we will "be with the Lord," it is clear that when He returns in the *final* phase of His coming of which Zechariah speaks, we will, in fact, be among "all the holy ones with him" when He stands on the Mount of Olives on that great day!

Let's sing it with vibrancy! Let's live with expectancy! Jesus is coming again! Maranatha! "Even so, come, Lord Jesus!"

ABOUT THE AUTHOR

John P. Moran, D.D., has served in the Missionary Church, Inc. as a missionary to Nigeria, a pastor for three churches and as the president of the denomination. He has also served as an evangelist and Bible teacher in local church and area crusades, camps and conferences in the U.S., Canada, Nigeria, Mexico, Brazil, the Dominican Republic, Puerto Rico and Spain. He is the author of JOY IN A ROMAN JAIL, a devotional exposition of Philippians.